What Was That?

He fled up the stairs, through the kitchen, up another flight, and down the hall. He flew into his bedroom, slammed and locked the door behind him, turned on one, two, all the lights, and, shaking, crawled into bed, face to the wall. I'm going crazy, he thought, panting. Then, no, I'm dreaming. That's it, I'm still asleep and I ...

Squeak.

Cold enveloped the room. Oh my God, what was that?

Squeeeeeak.

Bart's blankets were sheets of ice. He didn't want to turn around, but he had to. He did it slowly, his eyes darting wildly around the room. Finally, they hit on the closet door. It was open about an inch. As he stared, it slid open an inch further.

point

GHOST HOST

Marilyn Singer

SCHOLASTIC INC.
New York Toronto London Auckland Sydney

The author wishes to thank the following for service above and beyond the call of duty: Steve Aronson, Howard Altman, Carl Bivins, Mary Gunning, Donn Livingston, Terry Moogan, Hopi Morton, Asher Williams.

ISBN 0-590-44505-7

12 11 10 9 8 7 6 5 4 3   1 2 3 4 5/9

Printed in the U.S.A.   01

First Scholastic printing, September 1988

To Bill Aronson

GHOST HOST

Chapter 1

Sprocketsville wasn't a large town, but it did have its fair share of big, old, spooky houses. The biggest, oldest, and spookiest of them was 1351 Hexum Road. It had twelve rooms, including one that had been boarded up for three decades, a damp root cellar, and a musty, cobwebby attic. But Bart Hawkins had lived there for two whole years before he discovered that the place was haunted.

There'd been a lot of joking about ghosts and the like when Bart and his family moved into the house. Everybody had a story about the crazy Koral family, who'd owned the place for over seventy years. There was one about Old Man Koral, who'd supposedly buried treasure somewhere in the house; another that told of beautiful, tragic Lydia Koral, who died of a broken heart in Bart's bedroom. There were tales of loony spinster aunts, jealous lovers, even a batty beagle that pined away when its mistress died. "Every full moon, you can hear it howling behind that boarded-up door," somebody said.

It wasn't long before the Hawkins family realized that nobody was really serious about the eerie yarns. And once the house was cleaned and polished, painted and redecorated, the Hawkinses pretty much forgot about them — especially when no howling beagle, tragic young Lydia, or any other spirit showed up. The townspeople still cracked jokes about the place, but it was all in good-natured fun.

Bart's friends in particular got a lot of mileage out of ghost gags. Bart didn't mind, because he wasn't the type to believe in ghosts.

That's what he told his friends — and especially his girlfriend, Lisa. Just one week before Bart was about to have his disbelief proved totally wrong, he and Lisa went to see *Scare Tactics*. For most of the film, Lisa had her head buried in Bart's shoulder. When it was over and they were on their way to Yumby's for a snack, she said, "Ooh, that was so creepy. Wasn't it creepy?"

Bart smiled. "Not really," he said.

"But Bart, that scene where the guy was shaving and the ghost steps out of the shower . . ."

"Good special effects."

"All right, but what about when the girl checks everywhere in her room — the closet, the wardrobe, under the bed — but she doesn't look *in* the bed itself and the ghost is there? When she screamed I almost died!"

"Good acting."

They walked into Yumby's. A buzz of excitement greeted their arrival, which wasn't surprising. After all, Bart was dark, good-looking, and the only junior in over twenty years to become star quarterback of the Dr. Kelley DeForest High School football team. The year before, he'd led the sophomore team to a stunning victory. Hopes were high he'd do the same this year for the varsity, a team that had finished last or next to last three years in a row. Bart's hopes were higher than anyone else's. He wanted to win. He had to win. It was the winners everyone liked, not the losers.

Bart knew that all too well. He'd been one of the losers. For years Bart was never much interested in sports, even though his father, a rabid football fan, tried to get him to be. He was much more interested in books. He read them by the stack, often choosing tough ones to challenge himself. Sometimes in school he'd give reports on them or even quote from them in class. The other kids thought this was a little weird, but they might have ignored it if Miss Kaminsky, Bart's sixth grade teacher, hadn't noticed and made him her pet. Being a teacher's pet in Bart's sixth grade equaled being the biggest loser of all time. The other kids, branding him a nerd, teased him mercilessly and shunned his company.

His reputation followed him into seventh and eighth grades. In desperation, Bart finally took up football, much to his father's delight, and he discovered he had a knack for it — and for basketball and baseball as well. Then the Hawkinses moved to Sprocketsville. No one knew about Bart's past — and he was determined they wouldn't find out. Oh, he'd do well enough in school to get decent grades, but Bart the Bookworm was dead — at least to all appearances — and Bart the Big Man was born.

"You really weren't scared?" Lisa asked, ignoring the Yumby's crowd in her exasperation with Bart. She was no slouch in the popularity department either, being cute, friendly, the captain of the cheerleading squad, and the vice president of the junior class.

He smiled at her again and stroked her cheek. "You know I don't believe in ghosts," he said.

"You don't?" a male voice cut in. "Then who was that vision I saw you with last night?"

"Vision? What vision?" asked Lisa.

"Blond hair, blue eyes. Why . . . why, I do believe . . . yes . . . yes . . . it was you!" Greg Spinetti said in a theatrical voice.

"Oh, cut it out." Lisa blushed.

The three of them headed over to a booth in the corner where two other guys, Bob Lucas and Tony Martini, were sitting. On the way, Bart was greeted by ten other kids, six of them girls.

"Hi, Bart."

"How's it going, Bart?"

"Great game today, Bart!"

"You really faked out the Rockets with that handoff."

Bart nodded and smiled at each of them.

"So, what's new, Hawkins?" Bob asked when he and Lisa finally squeezed in next to him.

"He doesn't believe in ghosts," Greg put in.

"You don't, huh?" said Bob.

"No, I don't. That silly stuff's for kids," Bart said.

"Well, I believe in them. And I'm not a fool," Lisa said.

"I'm with Bart," said Tony. "But then again, if *I* lived in the old Koral place . . ."

"You'd be a ghoul," Greg finished.

Everyone groaned.

The waitress arrived and took their order, and the talk turned to football. They spent a long time picking apart the day's game, which had been a tough and satisfying victory for their team — their fourth win and the second time they'd beaten the Rockets.

"Next week'll be even tougher," said Bob, the Phantoms' middle linebacker and kicker, as their food arrived. "The Rockets have a great offense, but their defense isn't so good. But the Red Devils have good offense and defense. We beat 'em last time. . . ."

"And we'll beat 'em again," Tony, a halfback, said. "We'll smash 'em to bits, and then we'll mash what's left over."

"Right! The Phantoms forever!" Lisa yelled. "Hooray for the Hawk!" She looked at Bart.

The rest of the kids in the restaurant cheered with her.

Bart smiled generously at them all like a king

bestowing his royal presence among the masses.

"You were terrific today, Bart," Gillian Landers said, pausing at his booth. It was no secret that she had an enormous crush on him. "Good luck next week. It's going to be a great game."

"We know you'll win," added Rosemary Rushing, Gillian's friend and another of Bart's admirers.

"Thanks," he said.

They hung around a moment, hoping for another word from him.

But it was Lisa who said, "Don't forget to bring your pompoms. We want to show the Devils just how many fans we've got."

"We will," Gillian and Rosemary chorused, but still didn't move.

So Lisa went on, "We could use some help for the dance afterward too. It's going to have a Halloween theme. Kristi says there aren't enough people on the decorating committee. Maybe you two would be interested...."

"Uh..." said Gillian.

"Well..." said Rosemary.

"Great. And there's Kristi now. You can go right over and talk to her about it."

Gillian and Rosemary, looking a little crestfallen, had no choice but to do just that.

"This girl never stops working," Tony teased.

"Or keeping other girls away from her man," added Greg.

"Oh, stop," Lisa said. "Kristi does need help

—and those two girls might enjoy some company besides their own for a change."

"They sure would — Bart's. Hey, Bart, you wouldn't consider asking someone else to this dance, would you? Then you could give the rest of us a chance."

"A chance at what?" asked Bart.

"A chance with Lisa," Greg said, wiggling his eyebrows at her.

"Fat chance," she said.

"Yeah, Greg's right." Tony turned to Bart. "It's a Halloween dance. You can go with one of the ghosts from that haunted house you live in."

"The tragic Lydia," said Bob.

"Or the baying beagle," offered Greg.

"Lisa wouldn't be jealous of a ghost, would you?" Tony teased.

"She ought to be. A ghost would be a better dancer."

"What?" Lisa squeaked. "How come?"

"Because it's lighter on its feet."

"Ohhh," everybody groaned again.

"Somebody stuff a yumburger in his mouth," said Bart. Little did he know it was the last time he'd be able to stand any ghost jokes for quite a while.

Bart walked Lisa home. "I can't see you tomorrow. I've got to study. Got an English test Monday. *Silas Marner.*"

"Ugh. I hate that book."

"Yeah."

Lisa gave him a mischievous look. "Yeah? I bet you haven't even begun to read it yet, right?"

"Well . . ." He smiled at her.

"Oh, Bart." Lisa looked at him and shook her head. "You football players," she said affectionately.

Bart didn't respond.

"I'll miss you tomorrow," she said.

"Yeah."

"Call me when you get bored with studying."

"Sure." He gave her a kiss and sauntered toward his house.

It was the last one at the bottom of the street. He looked up at it. Even after nearly two years of living there, he was still surprised by its size. The porch light was on and there was a light burning in his parents' bedroom. His older sister's window was dark — she was out on a date. His younger brother's room wasn't visible from the front of the house, but it was probably dark too, since Dusty would already be asleep. Then Bart looked at his own window and blinked. A tiny glow passed behind it, flickering like a candle flame, only silver. He blinked again. The light was still there. If Dusty's messing around in my room again I'll kill him, Bart thought. He quickly unlocked the front door, went up the stairs to his room, and opened the door.

It was pitch black and very cold. He shivered, flicked on the light, and looked around. Nothing seemed to be out of place — except for the copy of *Silas Marner* he'd left lying on the floor. He picked up the book, put it on his desk, and shivered again. It felt like the air conditioner was going full blast. But Bart's had been broken since August. He checked it anyway. Not running. He looked at the windows. One was open. But it was a balmy night out, and the slight breeze couldn't have chilled the room so much. He shrugged and shut the window anyway. Then he changed into his pajamas and went to the bathroom to brush his teeth. He heard a faint bang coming from his room. He rinsed his mouth and hurried back. The room was still icy, and the book was lying on the floor again. He picked it up and glanced at it. It was a different book this time. The title stared up at him: *The Haunting of Hill House.* "All right, Dusty. Where are you?" He poked around his room, looking in the closets, under the bed and the desk, behind the curtains. No one was there. He strode down the hall until he got to his brother's room. He carefully opened the door. He couldn't see well in the dark, but his ears were greeted by the unmistakable sound of Dusty's snoring.

He tiptoed over to the bed. In a low voice, he said, "You don't fool me, kid. I've told you ninety-eight times to stay out of my room. This is number ninety-nine. Once more and I take drastic measures."

In answer, Dusty snored louder.

Bart left his brother's room and went back to his own. "Brr," he said to himself. He shut off the light, climbed into bed, and pulled the covers up to his chin. He fell asleep so fast he didn't see a silvery glow shimmering near the stand-up mirror.

Chapter 2

"Ninety-five, ninety-six, ninety-seven, ninety-eight, ninety-nine, one hundred." Bart shook his fingers. Massaging his scalp was almost as much of a workout for his hands as the exercises he did to improve his grip. But hand exercise wasn't the reason for the scalp treatment. Bart had read in a magazine that massaging the scalp prevented hair loss. His dad had begun balding at age twenty-three, and Bart didn't want to find himself in the same predicament. He had a recurring nightmare about it. There he was, star quarterback of the Jets. The Jets were behind twenty-seven to twenty-one with ten seconds to play, third down and the ball on their own forty-yard line. He called the signals, "Blue, Monday, forty-six. *Hut* one! *Hut* two!" He got the snap and faked a handoff to the halfback, who ploughed through the line. He faded back and looked for his receivers. They were all covered. The Jets' line was beginning to break. Twelve hundred pounds of Chicago Bears were bearing down on him. Suddenly he saw his half-back in the clear on the ten-yard line. He uncorked a long one. It spiraled, arced, and landed perfectly in the halfback's outstretched hands. Touchdown! They won the Super Bowl!

He was carried off the field into the locker room, where scores of reporters were waiting to interview him. He flashed them a big smile, pulled off his helmet, started to run a hand through his thick, brown hair, and froze. There wasn't a hair on his head.

"Eww, look at that!" one reporter called out. She began to giggle. The rest of the reporters joined in.

"FOUND ME OUT," a loud voice rang in Bart's brain. He stuck his helmet back on his head and bolted from the room, the laughter following him all the way out of the stadium.

The first time he had the dream, he awakened shuddering, and after two days of research, began doing his scalp routine daily.

Besides the massage, the routine consisted of a once-a-week dousing with a special formula Bart had dug up from another magazine. It was a combination of herbs and other things. He would rub the stuff in and let it sit for ten minutes. Then he would wash it out. He was just about to open the medicine cabinet to get the mixture when the bathroom door flew open and a smaller version of Bart barreled into the room.

"Whuff!" exhaled Bart as Dusty tackled him.

His head missed the bathtub's hard edge by inches.

"You jerk! You could've killed me!" Bart said, sitting up.

"Not really," said Dusty. "The distance between where you were standing and the tub is seven feet, four inches. You're five eight. If an object with the velocity of three miles an hour and the mass of seventy-seven pounds strikes a —"

"Spare me," groaned Bart. The fact that his eleven-year-old brother was a mathematical genius wouldn't bother him if only Dusty would keep that fact to himself. It was also the only area in which Dusty was a genius. In every other way he was just a pesky little kid.

"Did I interrupt your beauty routine?"

"My scalp treatment. And listen, Dustmop, I've got something to say to you. I meant it when I told you last night that if you mess around once more in my room, I'm really going to clean the floor with you." He stared narrowly at his brother.

Dusty returned the stare, but his eyes were puzzled. "Huh?" he said. "I haven't been in your room since last week when you told me to get your sweatshirt."

"Come off it. You were there last night, dumping my books on the floor. I don't know how you got the air conditioner to work or what you did to get the room so cold, but you must've done something."

Dusty's look of puzzlement didn't change. "No, I wasn't and I didn't," he said.

Bart stood up menacingly. "You're getting me angry, kid. First you do what I told you not to and then you lie about it."

"I'm not lying about it, Bart. Honest, I'm not," Dusty said, suddenly looking a bit scared.

Something in his face made Bart think he might be telling the truth. But he didn't want to back down so easily. "Remember, once more . . ." he threatened. Then he turned to the medicine cabinet and opened it. A strong smell hit him and his eyes opened wide.

Everything in it had been turned upside down. A few of the tubes and bottles were leaking, among them Bart's precious hair formula, collecting in a sticky, odorous goo on the bottom shelf. He swore loudly, then turned to Dusty.

His brother was standing there giggling.

"You little . . ."

"I . . . didn't . . . do . . . that," Dusty gasped between giggles.

Bart reached for him. But Dusty slid under his arms and bolted out the door.

"Darn little poltergeist," Bart said, and wondered why that word had come to his lips.

After he'd cleaned up the mess in the bathroom as best he could, Bart went downstairs to the kitchen.

The rest of the Hawkins clan, except for his father, who was fetching the Sunday paper from the porch, were already there waiting for him. One of Mrs. Hawkins' rules was that on Sunday mornings the entire family had to breakfast together. Bart could practically hear their stomachs rumbling impatiently.

"Well, if it isn't the big football hero at last," Leanne, his older sister, sneered. She was thin and angular, just like their mother, and her temper was thin and angular too.

Bart ignored her. "Sorry I'm late, Mom," he said. "There was an . . . uh . . . accident in the bathroom." He glared at Dusty, but his younger brother wasn't looking at him. He had his nose buried in a copy of *Mathematical Games and Puzzles*.

"There's always an accident in the bathroom the minute you set foot in it," Leanne said.

Once again Bart pretended he didn't hear her. "What's for breakfast?"

"Pancakes," his mother answered from her place at the stove. "Cranberry with a soupçon of orange peel." Mrs. Hawkins was always using fancy words — especially when she needed to swear. She never used foul language — instead she'd just scream out words that sounded nasty but were perfectly decent, such as *pismire* or *bastinado*.

"Orange peel soup?" Bart said.

"No, dear. A soupçon is a small amount, a dash."

"Oh."

"Now we know for sure what Bart has under his helmet — a soupçon of brains." Leanne laughed snidely.

This time Bart whirled on her. "What's eating you this morning, Donuthead?" he said, using a nickname he'd given her years ago when he caught her polishing off a whole package of French crullers.

She turned a splotchy red. "I'll tell you what's eating me. Next time you borrow my albums without asking and wake me in the middle of the night to return them, I'll leave a surprise for you in your football helmet you won't forget."

"Huh?" Bart stared at her openmouthed. "What are you talking about?"

"Don't give me that. Something woke me up at about three o'clock. Then there was a thump and my door slammed shut. I turned on the light and saw my Ghostriders albums all over the floor. It's a wonder I didn't slip on them and break my neck, you turkey."

"Leanne!" Mrs. Hawkins said sharply.

"I didn't touch your dumb records," Bart insisted. "I don't like the Ghostriders and I wasn't even awake then."

Suddenly, he turned his head and looked at Dusty. In a moment Leanne did the same.

Dusty was still reading his magazine. Leanne plucked it out of his hands. He shrank down in his seat. "Hey, leave me alone. I didn't do anything. I didn't take your records, Leanne. And I told you before, Bart, I didn't mess with your books either."

"Your books? What does he mean your books?" Leanne turned to Bart.

Bart was still looking at Dusty. And now he was sure Dusty was telling the truth. "Nothing. A misunderstanding," he said.

Dusty shot him a grateful glance.

Then Mr. Hawkins walked into the room. He was carrying the Sunday paper in his arms. Or what was left of it. It had been neatly shredded into long, thin strips.

"Good grief," said Mrs. Hawkins. "What happened to the paper?"

"If you know, then tell me and we both will," Mr. Hawkins answered, frowning. "It was lying on the porch just like that."

"Oh well, we'll have to go down to Yarnell's and get another one."

"If there are any left," Mr. Hawkins groused. The Sunday paper was his weekend treat because it had the best sports section, which was the only part he read all the way through. He tossed it into the garbage pail and sat down at the table. Mrs. Hawkins handed him a cup of coffee and began to dish up the pancakes. Mr. Hawkins took a sip of the coffee and sighed. He was a big, goodnatured man who rarely got into a bad mood. But when he did, they "knew about it all the way to the North Pole," as Mrs. Hawkins liked to say.

He took another sip and looked up with a smile at Bart. "That was some game yesterday," he said. "Nine completed passes out of twelve."

"Yeah," Bart answered.

"What does that bring your total for the season up to?"

"Forty-two."

"Great!"

"That means if you get an average of six point six six, rounded off to the nearest hundredth of course, completed passes for the remaining three games, you'll break Flip Walonski's record," Dusty announced, naming Sprocketsville's football legend.

Mr. Hawkins frowned slightly at him. Dusty's mathematical abilities tended to unnerve him a bit.

"Dad, I forgot to tell you. The Jazzettes are performing in the talent show," Leanne said suddenly. The Jazzettes were a rock group, and she was the lead singer.

"That's wonderful!" Mrs. Hawkins said.

"Yeah. Very nice, very nice," said Mr. Hawkins. "So, Bart . . ." He turned back to his son without noticing that his daughter was glaring at both of them. "It's a beautiful day out. How about going jogging today with your old man? A quarterback can never get in too good shape, eh?"

"Uh, not today, Dad," Bart answered. "I've got to study."

"Study? Study for what?"

"For an English test."

"Ha!" snorted Leanne. "I thought you've given up studying."

"What do you have to study for? You don't need an 'A' in English to get a football scholarship." Mr. Hawkins was only half joking, and

Bart knew it. His bookishness had always made his father uncomfortable.

"That's true," Bart said calmly. "But I do need to pass it."

"Leave Bart alone," Mrs. Hawkins said. "I think it's excellent that he's going to study. He used to study all the time. And read." She looked at her son. "Remember how many books you used to read each week? I wish you still did that instead of being so wrapped up in football. Lord knows, football won't get you anywhere in the real world."

Mr. Hawkins looked at his wife as if it were Super Bowl Sunday and she'd just told him she'd sold their TV. "Tell that to Joe Namath," he said.

Or to the kids at DeForest High, added Bart silently. But he felt a twinge of regret. His mother looked sad; she was mourning the death of Bart the Bookworm. I wish I could tell her the truth, he thought. That the Bookworm isn't really dead. He's only . . .

"Is there any more maple syrup, Mom?" Dusty asked, interrupting his thoughts.

"I'll check." She got up and walked through a small side door into the pantry.

"Well, I'm finished," said Leanne to no one in particular. She stood up too, picking up her plate.

Suddenly, Mrs. Hawkins' voice blared out from the pantry, "Crepuscular!"

Leanne dropped her plate. It cracked neatly down the middle.

Mr. Hawkins jumped to his feet, knocking his chair over. "Maura, are you okay?"

The pantry door swung open and Mrs. Hawkins stood there, her hands smeared red.

"Maura! Oh my lord! Quick, run them under cold water. Leanne, get the bandages. . . ."

"That doesn't look like blood," Dusty said, going over to his mother. "It looks like — "

"Jam. Red currant jam. Every da—I mean, every wretched jar of the stuff is broken. And you know how many jars we put up from that blasted bush?"

"Twenty-seven," said Dusty. "We all got sick of the stuff."

Mrs. Hawkins squinted at her family. "Okay. Who did it?"

"Don't look at me," said Leanne.

"Uh-uh." Dusty shook his head.

Bart didn't say anything. He was thinking of the medicine cabinet.

"Bart?"

"Huh? Oh no, Mom. I wouldn't do anything like that no matter how sick of red currant jam I got."

"Somebody's not telling me the truth," Mrs. Hawkins said tightly.

"Now Maura, just because we got sick of red currant jam doesn't mean any of us would go around smashing jars of it," Mr. Hawkins said soothingly. "Maybe they exploded. I thought I heard that jars can do that. Something to do with a vacuum . . ."

"The window was open. A cat could've gotten

in," Dusty offered. "Old Kingston was sniffing around here last night."

"A cat can't open a closed door."

"Maybe it wasn't closed all the way."

"What about an earthquake?" said Leanne.

"Yeah," agreed Dusty. "That would explain your records and Bart's books and even the medicine cabinet."

"The medicine cabinet?" said Mr. Hawkins.

"I don't know. I didn't feel any earthquake and I'm a light sleeper," Mrs. Hawkins said.

They were still listing possibilities when Bart left. He felt tense and irritable, and that was strange. He was usually relaxed and easygoing, especially on Sundays, the one day he could really call his own. True, there had been all those incidents — the medicine cabinet mess, the hassles with Dusty and Leanne, the newspaper and the jam — but now they seemed too minor for him to feel so bothered. Maybe it was that lie about my studying, he thought. But that didn't make sense — he'd lied before without that much anxiety. Besides, it wasn't really even a lie; he did have to study. However, he knew it wouldn't take very long — he'd already finished *Silas Marner* yesterday morning and he remembered it well enough without much studying. It wasn't even a bad book. He'd rather liked it. But he'd never tell Lisa that because she'd get suspicious. "You read it already? And you liked it? What are you, some kind of a bookworm?" she'd ask, in a playful manner to be sure, but Bart thought she wouldn't be so playful if she found out the answer to her last question was yes. And as for his family, he didn't want to tell them the truth either. Oh, they wouldn't care about one particular book. But they would care if they knew what Bart was really planning to do this afternoon. Especially his mother. She'd be so proud. She'd brag about it, the way she used to, and his name would be Barf instead of Bart. No, the lie was necessary, he thought. He dismissed it as the cause of his tension and continued on to his room.

Before he got there, he stopped at Dusty's. The door was open. One of his brother's mobiles, a bunch of little silver airplanes, was swinging in the gentle breeze blowing through the window. Bart felt himself grow calmer. The mobile looked like a nice thing to wake up to. He walked into the room for a closer look. Suddenly a blanket of cold wrapped itself around him. One of the planes snapped off the mobile and whizzed past his head. A second plane followed. A third. Bart stood there openmouthed as the planes swooped and dived around the room. He ducked as one nearly clipped his ear. I've got to get out of here, he thought, but he was unable to move his feet.

Then abruptly, all of the planes crashed to the floor. Bart stood there shivering. It was a long moment before he managed to pick up one of the planes and examine it. Metallic plastic with a tiny propeller. No motor. Not even the rubber band kind.

He heard a slight groan behind him. He whirled around. The bedroom door was closing. He stumbled toward it and flung it open.

"Dusty, you little . . ." he growled, running into the hall.

But no one was there. He dashed toward the stairs, then stopped short. It couldn't be Dusty. He wouldn't wreck his own mobile, Bart thought, even if he could.

Still shaking a little, he turned back toward his room, his mind running over the possibilities. None of them made much sense. Except one. And Bart didn't like that one at all.

Chapter 3

Bart's stomach grumbled. He glanced at the clock on his night table. Twelve-thirty. Lunchtime. His stomach was always punctual.

He closed his notebook. He had finished studying. Just as he'd expected, it hadn't taken very long. He'd even done his history assignment. The work had helped push unwelcome thoughts out of his head — even though it had been a struggle to sit down and do it. When he'd gotten to his room after the mobile incident, he'd slammed the door and sat on his bed, shaking. *Poltergeist*, he thought. This house has a poltergeist. But slowly, logic had taken over. There *had* to be a sensible explanation. Maybe Dusty had rigged something up to spook him. Or maybe there were some strange air currents in the room. But he hadn't sought out his brother or anyone else to ask. He'd just breathed slowly and deeply, a relaxation exercise he'd come across in a magazine, and turned to *Silas Marner*. And old Silas had been a good friend.

Bart stood up and walked to his door. But as soon as he put his hand on the doorknob, he began to feel weird again. What if it were there on the other side, waiting? His stomach spoke up again. *Borborygmus.* He remembered his mom using the word. It had made him laugh. What if *what* were waiting, dumbo, he said to himself. Coach Dibbetts telling you you've been cut from the team? Now that would be scary. This time he opened the door without any hesitation and started down the hall. As he neared Dusty's room he felt his shoulders tense. The door was ajar and he could see the remains of the mobile lying just as he'd left them. However, nothing else was amiss. Dusty hasn't been back up here yet, he thought, wondering if he should gather up the planes and put them somewhere. But he didn't want to go into the room, so he shut the door and went downstairs, taking the steps two at a time.

The house was quiet and peaceful. There was no sign of Dusty, Leanne, or their parents. On the one hand, Bart was relieved. He didn't feel like hassling with or lying to anyone again. And now he had the place all to himself to do what he'd planned to do all along. On the other hand, having the place all to himself didn't seem quite so pleasant anymore. He shook his head and was about to go back to his room when a chill wound itself around him. It was only a slight one, more a vague sensation than anything else, but suddenly Bart knew he couldn't stay in the house. He looked out the window. It *was* a beautiful day out. Hey, I don't have to do it inside, as long as I'm careful, he thought. And as long as I'm back in time to watch the Bears–Giants game.

He ran up to his room once more, his eyes avoiding Dusty's door. He grabbed a light jacket with deep pockets from his closet and threw it on. Then he rooted around under the stack of old *Tales from the Crypt* comics on his bookshelf, found what he was looking for, and shoved it into one of the pockets. As an afterthought, he stuck the copy of *Silas Marner* in another pocket, dashed down to the garage, got his bike, and pedaled away from his house as quickly as he could.

The shortest way to Rowan Woods was straight down Hexum Road, right on Ehler and left on Mason. But that would take Bart right past Lisa's house, so he chose a longer, less direct route, hoping that he wouldn't run into anyone he knew or who knew him.

His luck held until he was halfway there. Then he saw someone waving at him. It was Kristi South, Lisa's best friend, known not-so-affectionately to Bart as South the Mouth.

He groaned silently, gave her a big smile as he rode by, and immediately began to make up a series of explanations to give Lisa.

He was still working on them when he reached the thick stand of ash and oak trees. There were lots of parks and forested areas in and around Sprocketsville, but of all of them, Rowan Woods was Bart's favorite — partly because it wasn't as popular as the others and partly because there was a peeling log cabin there that Bart had often explored when he first moved to the town. Occasionally he still did, even though there was nothing much inside but broken-down furniture and a few candle stubs.

There was also a little creek that ran through the woods, and when the sunlight hit it just right it shone like a stream of diamonds. That was Bart's favorite place of all. He wheeled his bike toward it, put down the kickstand, found a wide, flat stone his rear end fit comfortably upon, and settled down. Then he reached into his pocket and pulled out what he'd hidden there. It was the play *Macbeth* by William Shakespeare. The cover showed a man with hooded eyes reaching for a ghostly dagger. Bart the Bookworm wasn't dead after all. And now, as he emerged from his hiding place, the Bookworm shouted, Free, free again, gave a little shudder of pleasure, and opened the book. He quickly skimmed the introduction, discovering with delight that the play supposedly had a curse on it. Then he turned to Act I, scene i, and began to read in earnest.

An hour and a half passed. Bart was only halfway through Act II of the five-act play. It wasn't an easy play to get through. He had to pause frequently to look up a word or a phrase in the footnotes or to try and make sense out of a sentence or even an entire speech. Sometimes he just couldn't. He knew he wasn't getting all of it, but it didn't matter, because what he did get was better than any Halloween tale he'd ever read. It was all about Macbeth, a nobleman who is told by witches he's going to be king. When he tells his wife what they said, she suggests they make it happen sooner by bumping off the present king, Duncan, and he does. Bart especially liked the part right before Macbeth kills Duncan, which the cover picture showed. Bart stood up with the play in his hand and began to read it out loud:

Is this a dagger which I see before me,
The handle toward my hand? Come let me
*   clutch thee.*

He reached out with his free hand.

I have thee not, and yet I see thee still.
Art thou not, fatal vision, sensible
To feeling as to sight?

He dropped his voice.

or art thou but
A dagger of the mind . . .

He stared ahead of him, almost expecting to see the imaginary knife.

What he saw instead was a pale, round face. And it was coming toward him.

He let out a yell, stepped backward, and tripped over a rock. He felt his left ankle twist as he hit the ground, and for a moment all he could do was lie there. Then, remembering the face, he scrambled to a sitting position.

The face was still there. It opened its mouth. "Are you okay?" it asked.

But this time Bart recognized it. It belonged to Arvie Biedemeyer, Dr. Kelley DeForest High School's chief nerd.

Chapter 4

Arvie was pudgy and freckled. He had curly brown hair, a squeaky voice with a crack in it, and a very small nose. He looked about three years younger than he was, which was something Bart, unlike some other kids, didn't find worthy of mockery. Nor did Arvie's incredible brain bother Bart. What *did* bug him was the way Arvie showed off that brain because, although he wouldn't admit it, Arvie reminded him a little too much of someone else Bart once knew: himself.

Just as in the past Bart had not kept his knowledge and his love of books to himself, Arvie liked to share what he learned with the world. When any teacher asked him a question, Arvie not only knew the answer, but he also knew more than the teacher. So Arvie's answers often turned into lectures, which he liked giving. He also liked doing long reports he could read out loud in class.

His last report had been for science. It was

on the psychological theories about the nature of personality, psychology being Arvie's special interest. It began: "Some people think it's harder for a person to change his personality than for a leopard to change his spots. Can a self-centered macho type really become a sensitive man? Can a painfully shy girl ever become a star?"

"Can a genuine nerd actually turn into a human being?" Greg Spinetti had stage-whispered to Bart, and the whole class had broken up.

Arvie hadn't laughed with them. He didn't understand why other people didn't find psychology or his other interests as fascinating as he did. Of course he didn't understand why they liked the things they did — football, for instance. Football was a mystery to him. Football players were strange too. But Arvie did try to make sense of them as, he put it, "examples of the team-player psychology."

One of his "examples" was now lying on the ground in front of him. "Are you okay?" he asked again.

Bart got to his knees. "Yeah, I'm fine, fine," he said. He stood up, putting his left foot down gingerly.

"I didn't mean to interrupt your performance." Arvie was holding Bart's book.

"It wasn't a performance."

"It wasn't?"

"No. I was just read— " Bart bit off his words. That's all he needed — the school nerd knowing his secret. "I was, uh, practicing, uh, voice projection. For football. Coach Dibbetts suggested it, so everyone can hear me loud and clear when I call the signals." Bart knew he was giving Arvie too much of an explanation, but somehow he couldn't stop himself.

Arvie nodded. "That sounds like a good idea. But how interesting that you were using *Macbeth* to practice with. Psychologically, that is."

Bart resisted the temptation to ask Arvie what the blazes he was talking about. Instead, taking the play from him and pocketing it, he said, "Yeah, well, see you around" and took a step toward his bike. "Oww," he said involuntarily.

"I don't think you're okay," said Arvie. "From here it looks like you sprained your ankle."

Bart stifled a nasty reply. "I guess I twisted it a little. It'll be okay. . . ."

"It's going to swell."

"No, it isn't," Bart said, but already he could feel the ankle beginning to balloon.

"Better soak it in cold water."

"Yeah, I'll do that as soon as I get home." He took another step and groaned.

"I think you ought to do it now. You're a football player. I don't know much about football, but at a guess I'd say you need to be able to use your feet."

This time Bart didn't bother to hold his tongue. His pleasant afternoon had turned into a throbbing ankle, a conversation with the school nerd, and a possible end to his football career. "Where? Where am I supposed to soak it? You got a bathtub handy?" he snapped.

Arvie didn't snap back. "You could try the creek," he said mildly.

Bart immediately felt like a jerk, but he tried to cover it up. "Bottom's muddy," he mumbled.

"Mud's good for a swelling too."

Bart didn't answer. He just began to limp toward the water.

"Need any help?" Arvie asked.

"No," Bart growled. He was feeling humiliated enough. To lean on the smaller guy's shoulder would be the last straw. "I can make it." He hobbled over to the bank, sat down, and eased off his sneaker and sock. He touched the ankle tenderly. Nothing broken. But it was turning red. He slid it into the cold creek and closed his eyes.

He sat that way for several minutes, his foot blissfully numb and his mind nearly that way too, until Arvie's squeaky voice startled him back to reality.

"Do you come here often?" he said.

"What . . . huh?" Because he was startled, he didn't think not to answer the question. "Uh . . . yeah . . . a couple of times a month at least."

"Funny, I've never seen you here before."

Bart wanted to close his eyes again and sit in silence, but curiosity got the better of him. "You come here a lot?"

"Oh, yes. Yes, indeed. I come here nearly every day."

"Every day? Why?"

"I'm communing with the spirit of my Great-Great-Great-Uncle Eustace Biedemeyer."

"Your uncle's a ghost?"

"Oh no. He's dead all right, but I think he took his psychic energy field with him."

Bart rubbed his forehead and closed his eyes again. He had no idea what Arvie was talking about, but whatever it was was starting to give him a headache.

"Great-Uncle Eustace was a psychologist. One of the first. My mother says that's where I get my interest in the workings of the mind." Arvie paused, waiting for Bart to say something. When Bart didn't, he continued. "By all accounts, Great-Uncle Eustace was an excellent psychologist, but his real passion lay in a different field — parapsychology, the study of psychic phenomena such as ESP, telepathy, and energy apparitions — otherwise known as ghosts."

In spite of himself, Bart found he was getting interested in what Arvie was saying. "Your great-uncle studied ghosts?" he said.

"Yes, among other things. He was also an amateur botanist, a writer, an inventor, and he played a mean fiddle."

For the first time Bart smiled at Arvie. "Sounds like a wild guy."

"Yes." Arvie nodded.

There was a pause, then Bart said, "But wait a minute. What does your Great-Uncle Eustace have to do with your coming to Rowan Woods every day?"

"Ah. Have you ever seen the log cabin here? It's about half a mile back in the woods."

"Yeah, I've seen it." Bart didn't care to mention the number of times he'd explored it.

"Well, that cabin belonged to Uncle Eustace. He lived there — and died there too."

"Right in the cabin?"

"Yes. He was a poor man when he died. He was spending more and more time and money studying parapsychology. He was firmly convinced ghosts do exist. Unfortunately, the American Academy of Psychology didn't agree with him. He was thrown out and forced to close down his practice. He spent his last few years devoting himself to his studies and to his inventions. He was working on something having to do with changing a ghost's energy field — or 'personality' — from negative to positive — or from 'bad' to 'good' — when he caught pneumonia and died."

Caught up in the story, Bart stared at Arvie. "Well — go on."

Arvie shrugged. "There's nothing more to tell. We inherited the cabin and the woods, but we left the land open to the public. I like to come here because I see my great-uncle as my mentor, my guide. I like to talk with him — even though he's not here." He stopped talking.

Bart kept looking at him. The kid was a nerd all right, but he wasn't a total bore. Bart turned back to the stream.

After several more minutes passed, Arvie asked, "So how's your foot?"

Bart blinked and lifted his leg from the water. His whole foot was pink, but it was only slightly swollen and it felt a lot better. "Okay. Pretty good."

"Cold water and mud. A good combination."

Bart snorted, dried his foot with his sock, and then put the sock and his sneaker back on. He stood up. His foot *was* better. "Well, I've gotta go. . . ." He limped only slightly on the way to his bike. When he reached it, he turned to Arvie. "Uh . . . sorry I growled at you before. . . . And thanks for the advice."

"Don't mention it."

"Uh . . . yeah. Well, there's something I'd like you not to mention."

"Oh?"

"Yeah. Don't tell anyone you saw me here today. Okay?"

A funny, sad smile crossed Arvie's face. "Oh, don't worry. I won't."

"Thanks. I appreciate it." Bart wheeled his bike away.

And as he did, he heard Arvie mutter, "There's nobody to tell it to anyway."

Chapter 5

The Bears–Giants game was already eight minutes into the second quarter by the time Bart got back to his house. Soaking his foot had taken time, and the sore ankle didn't allow him to pedal his bike very fast.

His father was posted in front of the TV in his favorite chair. "Whaddja do, stick your hands in a bucket of grease?" he yelled at the Giants' fullback, who'd just fumbled the ball. Then he heard Bart and turned his head. "Well, there you are. Greg was here for a while, but he left when you didn't show. Where'd you go? I thought you were going to be studying all day."

"I was. I . . . uh . . . it was so nice out I took my book to the woods." He pulled the copy of *Silas Marner* out of his pocket and held it up for his father to see, thinking he wasn't actually lying this time; he *had* taken the book to the woods.

His father nodded. "You finished studying now? Want to watch the rest of the game?"

"Yeah," Bart said. He walked over to the

sofa. His foot was hurting again, and pedaling the bike had made it worse, but he tried not to show it. He didn't succeed, however.

"Hey, are you limping?"

"No. Uh . . . well . . . yeah, just a bit. I . . . uh . . . hit a pothole and fell off my bike." That one was a lie, but Bart didn't want to tell his father what had really happened.

"That's just great! You better put some ice on it."

"It isn't swollen much," Bart said.

"Let me see." Mr. Hawkins made Bart roll up his pant leg. He prodded the ankle.

"Ouch," said Bart.

"Ice. And now. You sit. I'll get it."

While his father went to get the ice pack, Bart tried to focus on the game. My ankle's gotta be okay, he thought. It's gotta be.

Then the phone rang. Bart sighed and hobbled over to it. "Hello," he said.

"So, how's old Silas?" Lisa's voice said.

Bart stifled a sigh. He didn't feel like talking to Lisa right now. In fact, he didn't feel like talking to anybody. "Oh, hi, Lisa. Fine. I'm fine. I mean, he's fine."

"Did you finish studying?"

"Yeah. I did."

"Good." Lisa's tone changed. Bart wasn't sure why until he heard her ask, "When did you finish?"

South the Mouth had blabbed already. "Not too long ago." He didn't want to give her the same excuse he'd given his father. He knew she'd want to know why he hadn't asked her to come to the woods too so she could enjoy the scenery while he studied. He made sure his dad wasn't back yet and said, "I . . . uh . . . I had to take some time out to . . . uh . . . run an errand for my father."

"Oh." Her tone changed back to normal. "Well, you want some company now to watch the game with?"

All Bart wanted was to be alone, but he politely answered, "I don't think so, Lisa."

"You don't?" she asked, surprised. "Why not?"

Suddenly, he was tired of lying. "Because . . . because I hurt my ankle."

"Oh, Bart! Your ankle! Is it serious?"

"No. I don't think it's serious."

"How'd it happen?"

He shook his head. Back to lies again. This time he fed her the same one he'd given his dad.

"That's awful. They ought to take better care of the streets. I'm going to complain."

Bart didn't respond. Then Mr. Hawkins reappeared, a large ice pack in his hand.

"Lisa? I gotta go now and get iced up."

"Oh, Bart."

"Listen, do me a favor. Don't tell anyone, okay? I don't want to sit out practice tomorrow."

"But Bart, if your foot's sore . . ."

"Please, Lisa."

"Okay. I won't tell a soul. But take care of yourself."

"Thanks. I will. See you," Bart said, and hung up.

"You play on a bad ankle and you'll sit out permanently," Mr. Hawkins said, lifting his son's foot gently and applying the pack to it.

"I'll be okay, Dad. Really."

Mr. Hawkins grunted in reply.

They sat awhile in silence watching the game, but Bart's mind wasn't on it.

"Jeez, will you look at that? Second fumble by twenty-four. He keeps playing like that and they'll use his contract to line a hamster cage."

"Hmmm," said Bart. He shifted a little. The ice felt good — even better than the creek. Colder. Much colder. A little chill ran up his back. He shivered and, for some reason, looked across the room to the sideboard where his mother always kept a vase of fresh flowers. At present, it was filled with big orange and yellow chrysanthemums. "Football mums. That's what they're actually called," he remembered his mother telling him with delight a few days ago when she'd bought them. He smiled at the memory. But his smile quickly faded. One of the mums was growing. Taller and taller, it pushed its way out of the vase. A second one followed. In another moment both of them would topple from the vase.

"Go! Go!" his father suddenly yelled. "He did it!" His shout distracted Bart, who glanced at the TV in time to see the Giants' fullback spike the ball and do a little victory dance in the Bears' end zone.

He whipped his head back to the vase and saw a perfectly normal bouquet of flowers sitting quietly in place.

Bart rubbed his eyes. What the devil was going on here? All of the day's events came back to him full force — the medicine cabinet, the jam, the mobile — especially the mobile. And now the flowers that grew or didn't. He looked at the vase again.

"Hi. Who's winning?" Dusty's voice interrupted his thoughts.

"The Giants, would you believe," Mr. Hawkins answered as the halftime break began. He got up and left the room.

"Great!" Dusty said. Then he noticed Bart's foot. "What happened to you?"

"Bike accident," Bart said. He peered up at his younger brother. "Uh, did you just come in?"

"Yeah. I've been in the yard working on a neat puzzle. If two trains run on parallel tracks, one at fifty miles per hour, the other at . . ."

Dusty was acting strangely unperturbed.

"Have you been up to your room since this morning?" Bart asked.

"I was up there an hour ago."

"Well, I didn't do it," Bart said.

"Huh?"

"I swear I didn't."

"That's good," said Dusty, looking at his brother as if he were nuts. "Listen, are you still mad at me about your books or something? Because if you are . . ."

"I'm not mad at you. I thought you'd be mad at me."

"About what?"

Bart blinked. Either this conversation was crazy or he was. "Your mobile, for pete's sake."

"What mobile?"

"The airplane one. The little silver airplanes."

"What are you talking about?"

Bart's hand closed on the ice pack. He wanted to chuck it at his brother's head. "It's ruined, isn't it? All the planes flew around and smashed to the floor while I was watching. But I didn't touch it."

It was Dusty's turn to stare. "Are you feeling okay, Bart?" he asked. "I mean, you didn't hit your head when you fell?"

"No, I didn't hit my head and it happened before I . . ." He bit off his words. He got unsteadily to his feet and started out of the room.

"Hey, shouldn't you keep off that foot?" Dusty called.

Bart ignored him. He made it to the stairs and hobbled carefully up them and down the hall until he got to Dusty's room. The door was closed. Without hesitating, he turned the handle and looked in.

The late afternoon sun streaming through the window lit up the room, sending a pattern of rays across Dusty's ceiling. Dangling there, shiny, silver, and all in one piece, was the airplane mobile twirling slowly in the October breeze.

Chapter 6

"Keep those legs up. I said *up*, Spinetti. You too, Lucas. No pain, no gain," Coach Dibbetts bellowed. "Okay, lower 'em. Over on your bellies. Time for the dead body drill. Hawkins, you're first."

Bart got up. It was his first day of practice after being disabled for three days. He hadn't succeeded in hiding his injury from the coach. He jumped over Greg, lying flat on his stomach, then over Bob Lucas, and so on down the line. When he'd leaped over the last guy, he flopped down on his belly to let Greg take his turn.

"Good going, Hawkins. Looks like the ankle's fine."

"It was fine yesterday," Bart grumbled, but he was pleased to be off the bench. Things were finally back to normal. Not only in terms of his ankle, but in his house too. There'd been no weird incidents for three days, and Bart had just about convinced himself that the stuff that had happened was the result of an earthquake after all.

Practice continued with passing and blocking. Then Coach Dibbetts gathered everyone around to teach them two new plays for tomorrow's game. "Got 'em, Hawkins?" he asked when he finished.

"Got 'em," Bart answered, and went over everything the coach had said.

They ran through the plays.

"Okay," said the coach. "I'll see you guys tomorrow at one-fifteen sharp. Go home and eat your carbs."

As the team headed for the showers, Greg fell in step alongside Bart. "Glad you're back in shape," he said. "Without you this team's got about as much chance of winning the championship as a snowbank in the Sahara. Coach Dibbetts ought to take out insurance on your hands and feet."

Bart grinned. "You're not such a bad player yourself," he said.

"I'm a damn good player. But I couldn't pull this team together the way you have. How do you do it? What do you do in your spare time, read books like *How to Be One Hell of a Leader*?"

Bart grinned again, but this smile wasn't so genuine. "Sure. I read books like that every single day."

Greg chuckled. "I'll bet. Anyway, don't mind me. I'm just jealous. If anyone has it all, you do, buddy — brains, brawn, and beauty."

"Beauty?"

"Yeah — Lisa. She doesn't have a sister just like her she's been hiding, does she?"

"Well, as a matter of fact, she does — her name is Jacey."

"Yeah?" Greg's eyes widened.

"Yeah. She looks just like Lisa. She's smart too, and her figure . . ." Bart paused.

"Keep talking," Greg urged.

"Her figure's great — for a twelve year old."

"Pow." Greg faked a right cross at Bart. They neared the entrance to the school. "Then again, maybe twelve isn't so young after all. I haven't had much luck with older women."

Bart didn't laugh. He sensed the undercurrent of frustration in his friend's joke. Greg really did want a girlfriend, but so far he'd struck out with the girls he'd dated. At the same time he felt sympathy for Greg, Bart felt lucky about and proud of his own success with girls. "Ah, just you wait, Spinetti," he said. "The right one will show up any day now, jogging across your path."

At that moment someone did jog across Greg's path. It was Arvie Biedemeyer.

"Hey Arvie. You trying to make running back?" Tony called to him as he puffed and panted along.

"Maybe he wants to be a cheerleader," Bob responded. "Hey, Arvie. *Yoohoo*, Ar-vie!"

Arvie looked up, spotted Bart, waved, and almost collided with a girl walking in the opposite direction.

Everyone laughed.

"What a nerd," said Greg, with a tone that suggested his own problems were minor compared to Arvie's.

"Yeah," Bart agreed, but he felt a faint twinge of discomfort as he said it.

He showered, changed, and picked Lisa up outside the girls' locker room. She'd just finished cheerleading practice.

"Well?" she asked, her blue eyes wide with expectation.

"Well, Coach Dibbetts has declared me ready, able, and more than willing to take on the Red Devils."

"Yippee!" Lisa said, throwing her arms around him and planting a big kiss on his lips.

"Ummm, maybe I should recover from injuries a little more often."

"Very funny," Lisa said. "Want to go to Yumby's?"

"I can't, Lisa," Bart answered. "I have to study."

"Again?"

"Spanish quiz." This time he didn't feel the least bit guilty, because not only did he really have a test coming up the next day, but Spanish was his worst subject and he needed all the studying he could get in.

"You better watch out, Bart Hawkins. With all the studying you're doing lately you're going to turn into another Arvie Biedemeyer," Lisa teased.

Bart smiled and didn't say anything.

They began to walk home.

"You know, I feel sorry for poor Arvie," Lisa said, more seriously. "He's awfully smart, and he's kind of cute, even though he looks about thirteen. But he just doesn't know how to . . . how to . . ."

"Be cool," Bart finished for her.

"Well, that's one way to put it. But it's more like nobody taught him how to act around people his own age or something."

"You sound like you wouldn't mind doing the teaching," Bart teased her back, although he wasn't entirely pleased with this conversation.

"No, I wouldn't. But I think you'd make a better teacher. You're everything someone like Arvie would probably like to be, and you could help him out."

"No, thanks," Bart said, a little too sharply. Then, realizing Lisa had jumped at his tone, he smiled and said, "I'd rather spend my time doing other things." He kissed her nose.

Lisa accepted the kiss, but didn't say anything. Bart could tell she was still thinking about Arvie, probably hatching some scheme to turn him into Mr. Popularity. Tony was right. Lisa never stopped working. Her specialty was misfits. She wanted to help them all become happy and loved members of society. Bart poked fun at her, but he knew her feelings were genuine. Last month it had been Patty Wheeler, whom she'd helped with a new hairstyle and a babysitting job. The month before was Rachel Rodriguez, once the most timid girl he'd ever met, but now a majorette — all because Lisa had caught her practicing twirling in the park and talked her into trying out. Bart hoped she wouldn't really take up Arvie as her latest cause. He wanted to see as little of Arvie as possible.

"Happy studying," she said. "Get a good night's sleep tonight."

"Yes, Mom," Bart replied. "I'll eat my carbs too."

"See that you do," Lisa played along. She gave Bart a kiss and went into her house.

As he walked toward his, Bart thought about Lisa, as he often did. She was wonderful, so why didn't he tell her the truth about himself? But then the same answer always came back to him: Because although Lisa might like to help misfits, she sure as heck wouldn't want to go out with one.

He reached his house, opened the door, and was greeted by Leanne's voice whining from the kitchen, "Oh, Ma, come on. It's only ten miles away."

"But the road there is treacherous, especially late at night."

"So we'll stay over."

"Where?"

"With Rocky's Aunt Peggy. She lives right nearby."

"I've never met Rocky's Aunt Peggy."

"She's a nice lady, Mom. A teacher. You'd like her. You can talk with her on the phone."

"I just don't know. Bart will be all alone . . ."

"Ma, it's a gig. A *paying* gig. What am I sup-posed to tell the Jazzettes? 'I can't make it, girls. My mother wants me to stay home and take care of my sixteen-year-old brother.' "

Bart walked in just as Leanne finished her outburst. "Good afternoon," he said, non-chalantly raiding the cookie jar.

"We're having a discussion," Leanne said.

"Is that what it's called?"

"Bart, Grandma Beamer phoned. She's feel-ing a bit . . . stressed," Mrs. Hawkins said.

Bart forced himself to keep a straight face. Grandma Beamer was often feeling a bit "stressed." He nodded. "She wants you to go see her," he said.

"That's right. Dusty, your dad, and I are going down there right after your game tomor-row. I know you have a dance to go to and won't want to come. As you must have heard, Leanne has a performing engagement — "

"A gig," Leanne interrupted.

"That she wants to keep. But it means she'll have to stay the night in Folger, leaving you here all alone."

"I'll be fine, Mom," Bart said.

"Are you sure you won't be lonely? I know you're sixteen — "

"That's right, Mom. He's *sixteen*," Leanne cut in.

Bart snorted. She always stuck up for him when it meant getting her own way.

"Well, all right," Mrs. Hawkins finally said. "But let me speak to Roxanne's Aunt Peggy."

"I'll call her," Leanne offered, eagerly heading for the phone.

Mrs. Hawkins smiled at Bart. "I guess it's hard for me to admit that my children are growing up."

Bart smiled back at her. "You'll get used to it, Mom," he said.

A few minutes later, Leanne returned. "Okay, Ma. She's on the phone," she said.

Mrs. Hawkins went out.

"So, you've got a gig," Bart said.

"So, you've got the house all to yourself," Leanne responded. "You could have a pretty wild time."

Bart grinned. Now there, he thought, was an idea.

Chapter 7

"Okay. Swing pass on three," Bart said in the huddle. "Everybody remember that one?"

"No. What am I supposed to do?" Tom Brewster, the right end, asked.

Patiently, Bart told him. "Got it?" he asked.

"Got it," answered Tom.

"All right. Break!" Bart yelled, clapping his hands.

The team got into position on the Red Devils' twenty-five-yard line.

Bart barked the signals. "Forty-three, twenty-seven, fifty-nine. *Hut* one. *Hut* two. *Hut* three!" He got the snap and backpedaled, looking to the right end. Then he swerved and threw a long, hard pass to Greg Spinetti, the left end, who was in the clear on the five-yard line. Greg caught it cleanly and stiff-armed his way to the end zone for a touchdown. Bob Lucas kicked for the point after and made it.

The crowd roared. Four minutes later, the game ended and the crowd roared again. Final score: Phantoms, twenty-seven; Red Devils, ten.

"See, I told you we'd mash 'em," Tony said to Bob, Greg, and Bart in the locker room as he took off his shoulder pads. "We're five and one. We're going to breeze right into the championship."

"I wouldn't be so sure of that. You know who we face next week. The Blitzberg Bombers. I know we've beaten them once, but it was by the skin of our teeth," Bart said.

"Right. And after them, the Shamashugee Surgeons," said Bob. "You know how they got their name? They can cut anyone to ribbons."

"They sure cut us to ribbons last time," said Bart.

"Well, let's not get depressed, guys. Let's enjoy the sweet taste of victory," Greg said, "and go out and meet our adoring public."

Bart's parents and Dusty were waiting for him. "Fifty completed passes," Dusty said, quoting the new statistic.

"Good work, Bart," Mr. Hawkins said. "You're playing like a champion."

Mrs. Hawkins gave him a hug. "I'm glad your ankle's okay." Then she said, "We're leaving for Grandma's now. Don't forget to close all the windows tonight if it rains as it's expected to. There's a casserole in the refrigerator. All you have to do is heat it up. I'm expecting a call from Eleanor Nutley about opera tickets, so please take down the information. Got all that?"

"Sure, Mom," Bart said.

"Good. I think that's about it. Except that the light switch in the basement seems to be faulty. I had trouble getting it to work today. Oh, and don't touch the tutus."

"The what?"

"The tutus. The ballet costumes from Mademoiselle Corinne's Dance Studio. They needed some repair work and I offered to do it. Mademoiselle Corinne's students are giving a recital next week. The tutus are in a box in the rec room all ready for her to pick up on Monday."

"Okay, Mom. I promise. No tutu-touching." Dusty giggled.

"Come on, Maura. Let's get going. If we stay here any longer, your instructions will be as long as the NFL rule book," Mr. Hawkins said.

"Hyperbole is not necessary, Howard," Mrs. Hawkins said. "And anyway, I happen to be finished. Have fun at the dance tonight, Bart."

"I will. Tell Grandma I hope she's feeling better."

His family left, and he turned to find Lisa at his side.

"They're going to visit your grandmother?" she asked.

"Yes." He grinned.

"Doesn't she live way over in Buzzard?"

"Uh-huh." His grin widened.

"Then they're staying overnight."

"Right."

"Bart, why are you smiling like that?" Lisa's eyes lit up. "Oh. Oh, are you thinking what I'm thinking . . ."

"Yep. Party time," said Bart.

Bart looked terrific. He'd given his scalp a special treatment and dressed carefully for the dance. Since Halloween was only a few days away, this dance was a costume ball. Bart had picked out his outfit several weeks before. He was going as a king. But it was only as he put on his crown and looked at himself in the mirror that he decided which king he was. "Macbeth," he murmured, scowling darkly. "And Lisa will be Lady Macbeth. Heh-heh-heh." He gave an evil chuckle. Except he knew he couldn't tell Lisa who they were because then she'd ask where he got the idea for that and he'd have to explain. No, it would just be his private joke.

He slipped the cloak his mother had made for him around his shoulders and went to meet his queen.

Lisa was gorgeous, as he knew she would be, in a white gown, silver cape, and sparkling tiara. Every head in the room turned when they entered the gym.

"Oh," moaned Gillian Landers, standing in her ballerina costume near the refreshment table.

"Oh, oh," echoed Rosemary Rushing, also dressed as a ballerina.

"Lisa, you look fabulous!" Kristi South squealed over the loud rock music the deejay was playing. "You do too, Bart." She quickly whisked her friend away to one side of the gym, where the girls were congregated.

Bart joined the male population of DeForest High at the other side.

"Hey, if it isn't King Bart the First," Tony Martini, dressed as a hobo, greeted him. "Spinetti, Lucas, and I were just discussing your little upcoming party."

"Yeah, well, keep it down or it isn't gonna be so little," Bart hushed him.

Tony lowered his voice. "It seems Lucas here is bringing a 'little' treat."

"What is it?" Bart asked.

"Let's give him a hint," said Greg. He was wearing his football uniform with a sandwich board over it that read: *The End of the World Is Coming*. Bart laughed when he read it. "Four letters, beginning with 'b' and ending with 'r.' And what's in between is 'ee'–zy."

"Oh. Beer." Bart said. "Where'd you get it?"

"From my basement," Bob said. "We have a bunch of six-packs left over from the Labor Day picnic."

"Won't your parents miss them?"

"Nah. Once they put stuff in the basement they forget it's there. They've got enough junk down there to start their own secondhand store."

"So where'd you hide them?"

"Out in the bushes next to the gym entrance. We'll pick 'em up on the way to your house."

"If somebody else hasn't picked 'em up first,"

Greg said. "The bushes by the gym entrance aren't exactly top secret."

"What do you mean?" asked Bob and Tony simultaneously.

"He means a lot of people hide things there," Bart said.

"Sometimes even themselves," added Greg. "Remember when Danny Haney and Bridget Kearny disappeared from the last dance for three hours? Guess where Chapman found them."

"We'll be right back," Bob and Tony said, heading for the door.

"You're gonna have some party," said Greg. Then the deejay put on a slow record.

"See you later, pal," Bart said, patting Greg on the shoulder. He crossed the floor to Lisa.

"Oh," said Rosemary Rushing. "Isn't he gorgeous?"

"Oh. Oh, isn't he?" said Gillian Landers as Bart and Lisa, crowns aglitter, began to dance.

At a little after nine, Bart and Lisa were no longer dancing. They were wedged into a corner of the rec room couch in Bart's house, kissing. Also squeezed on the couch were Bob, Greg, and Kristi South, who were listening to the Wild Ones' newest l.p. and watching a horror movie on TV at the same time. Bob was opening cans of beer and passing them around.

"None for me," Kristi said. "If my parents get a whiff of that on my breath, I'm grounded for the week."

"That's okay, Kristi," Bob teased. "It'll leave more for the rest of us."

The other boys murmured approval.

"Hey, Lisa. You want any?"

"Wait till they come up for air," said Greg.

"Ha ha," Lisa said, patting her hair into place. "Yes, I do want some. You can have some too, Kristi. I've got some Binaca with me. It'll cover up any telltale mouth odors."

"No, I'll pass. It's warm. I hate warm beer."

"This is the part where he kills her with an ax," Bob was saying.

"Oooh, disgusting," said Lisa, burying her face in Bart's shoulder.

"Hey, turn up the music," said Tony, taking a big gulp of beer. "I like this tune." He jumped up and started to do a silly dance and nearly knocked over a chair in the process.

"Watch it, Martini," Greg warned. "You bombed already?"

Nobody noticed Bart's frown.

"Lisa, we better leave soon. My parents are going to pick us up at ten at the school," Kristi said.

"Your folks are picking up you and Lisa? Lisa lives just down the street," Greg said.

"I'm staying over at Kristi's tonight."

"Yeah? I thought Lisa was staying elsewhere tonight," Tony said.

"Shut up, Martini," Bart rapped out.

Tony shut up.

"Okay, we'll go soon, Kristi," Lisa said, ignoring him.

"Relax, girls," Bob said, opening another can. The beer foamed out and onto the couch.

"Jeez, watch it, you dope!" Kristi yelled.

Bart, still frowning, grabbed a roll of paper towels and tossed it to Bob. "Clean it up," he said. He was beginning to wonder if the party was such a hot idea after all.

"Bob's right, girls. The party is just beginning," Tony, who'd polished off three cans and was eyeing a fourth one, said. He tried to sound suave, but the loud belch he let out ruined it.

"Eww! Gross!" Lisa exclaimed.

"Don't you have to go back to the dance, Martini?" said Kristi. "I heard your parents tell you they were going to pick you up at ten too."

Tony's ears reddened, and everyone laughed. The Wild Ones album ended, and he busied himself with flipping it over.

All of a sudden, there was a loud knock on the basement door. Everyone froze.

"Who's that? And how'd they get in?" whispered Greg.

"Did you invite anyone else?" Kristi asked in a low voice.

"It's not your folks, is it?" Bob said worriedly.

"It better not be old Mr. Rollins," Lisa put in. "He's always complaining about noise. If he's called the cops . . ."

"The cops! In the house!" Tony yelled.

Kristi jumped up. "Where's the bathroom?"

"Everybody cool it," Bart said, his calm voice cutting through the panic. "I'll handle this."

Everyone turned to him at once. He looked

back at them and saw trust and admiration replace the fear on their faces. He rose regally. King Bart the First. "Martini, lower the stereo. Lucas, hide the beer."

They jumped into action, following his orders just the way they followed his signals on the football field. "And everybody else stay put." He strode to the stairs, his cape flaring out behind him, and climbed up. Behind him the room fell into dead silence.

My parents, Officer? he rehearsed, picturing a hefty policeman in front of him. They'll be back shortly. Yes, I have a few friends over. No, my parents don't mind. He reached the top of the stairs. Yes, we'll keep the noise down. Yes, thanks, it was a good game. Next week? We'll slaughter 'em. He took a deep breath and opened the door. "Oh hello, Officer, how did you . . ."

"Hi, Bart."

"Hello, Bart."

He blinked. Instead of a burly policeman, Gillian Landers and Rosemary Rushing were standing there in their ballerina costumes.

"We rang the bell over and over . . ."

"But nobody answered."

"Then we found out . . ."

"The door was open."

"Tony said . . ."

"There was a party."

"So we came."

They finished their overlapping speech and stared, moon-eyed, at Bart.

"Uh . . . oh, yeah. Sure. Come on in."

The two girls smiled gratefully. "Thanks!" they said, brushing against him as they walked down the stairs.

Bart followed and almost laughed when he saw his friends. They were all sitting, quiet and upright, watching TV. There wasn't a beer can in sight.

"Hi, Tony. Hi, Bob. Hi, Greg," said Gillian.

"Hi, Lisa. Hi, Kristi," added Rosemary.

"Why, if it isn't Detectives Landers and Rushing," Greg said.

A collective sigh of relief went around the room.

"Break out that beer again!" yelled Tony, running over to the stereo. "And let's boogie."

"All right!" Bob shouted.

"Bart," Lisa said sweetly, "I'm starved. What have you got to eat?"

"The usual stuff. Potato chips, pretzels, peanuts. . . . Why don't you bring us all a big bowl?"

"Why don't we go get it together?" She stood up and, taking Bart's arm, steered him out of the room and back up the stairs.

"Imagine Rosemary and Gillian getting up the nerve to crash your party," Lisa said as soon as they got to the kitchen. She laughed lightly.

But Bart could tell she wasn't all that amused. He toyed with the idea of teasing her about it, but he was just too tired — tired from his strenuous day and tired of the way his friends were acting. An image of himself, alone on the couch in the living room, reading *Macbeth*, came to him. He sighed and pushed it away. "I don't think they crashed it," he told Lisa straightforwardly. "I think Tony invited them."

"But he didn't say anything."

"You think he'd remember to tell us in the state he's in?"

"Oh, he's just having a little fun," Lisa said.

"Yeah," Bart said with clear annoyance.

Lisa looked at him quizzically. "Bart, what is it? Aren't you having a good time?"

No, I'm not. I'm having a lousy time. I want to be alone with a good book, Bart wanted to say. Instead, he said, "Sure I am. I'm having a . . ."

Crash!

"What was that?" he yelled.

"I don't know, but it sounded like it came from the rec room," Lisa answered.

"Jeez!" Bart raced out of the kitchen. He threw open the door, ran down the stairs, and stared.

The rec room was filled with ballerinas. Big, little, blond, brunette, red-haired ballerinas in electric blue, red, purple, and green. But only one of them, bulkier than the others, was still dancing. It was Tony in a hot-pink tutu that had a long rip down the side. Greg, the only non-ballerina in the room, grabbed him and held him still. The others were looking at something white and shiny scattered on the floor. It took Bart a few seconds to realize it was the remains of a ceramic lamp.

"We're sorry, Bart," Gillian said.

"Very sorry," Rosemary added, even though neither of them had broken it.

"Wh-what happened to the Sh-sh-sugar Plum Fai-ree?" Tony slurred.

"Shut up," Greg said.

"What's going on he — Oh no!" Lisa, appearing behind Bart, exclaimed.

Bart gave a look that silenced her at once. Then he turned back to the rest of his friends. "That's it," he declared in a frosty voice. "Party's over."

Chapter 8

Plink plink. Plink plink. Flap.

"Uhhh."

Plink plinkity plinkity. Rat-a-tat-tat. Flap flap.

"What the . . ." Bart sat up in bed, trying to focus his eyes in the dark room. He turned toward the window. The shade, buffeted by the wind, was flapping back and forth in rhythm with the rain hitting the window pane. *Don't forget to close all the windows tonight if it rains as it's expected to.* Bart heard his mother's voice in his head. "Oh great," he grumbled aloud. He slid out from under the covers and sat for a moment on the edge of the bed. Jeez, what a night, he thought, remembering his friends filing out the door silently — well, not so silently, in Tony's case — and himself sweeping up the shards of the lamp. There wasn't anything he could do about the ripped tutu. He didn't know how to sew. He could've asked one of the girls to do it, he guessed, but at the time he'd just wanted all of them gone — even Lisa. Why do they have to act so stupid, he thought. You could've told Bob and Tony not to bring the beer, another voice whispered in his brain. But that wouldn't have been cool. . . .

The shade flapped again. He stood up with a groan and shut the window. Then, opening his bedroom door, he went to check the other windows in the house.

He was down in the kitchen when he heard the bump. He stood still and listened. There it was again. A loud thumping. It was coming from the rec room. "Oh, jeez. Now what?" he said. He opened the basement door and flicked the light switch. But the light didn't go on. He tried it again and a third time. Then his mother's voice echoed in his head once more: *The switch in the basement seems to be faulty.* He sighed, went back to the kitchen, and fished a flashlight out of a drawer. He turned it on as he reached the basement door and started down the stairs.

Boorump. The sound came again.

A wave of cold hit him. The hairs on his neck prickled. He stopped dead, clutching the stair railing with one hand. The logic that had asserted itself the week before in his bedroom was failing. He shuddered.

King Bart. Bart the Hawk. Ha, he told himself. You're real brave, Hawkins. Wouldn't the Phantoms love to see their star quarterback now. He stood still another moment. Then, setting his chin, he edged down another step. It's probably just the boiler acting up, he thought. No, it's not on. The water heater then. Another step. There's got to be a logical explanation. Another step. There, I made it. He turned right into the room that housed the boiler and heater. He inspected them with the flashlight, but nothing seemed wrong. He walked out and on toward the rec room.

It was dark and quiet. He played his flashlight over the furniture, the bar, the stereo, the TV, the knickknack shelves. Nothing was wrong here either. Then he noticed a box in a corner lying on its side. A bit of frothy pink tulle spilled from it. It rustled gently. The tutus. Bart had put the box on a low table when he'd cleaned up.

It must've fallen off, he told himself. See, a logical explanation. And you let yourself get scared of . . .

Boo-rump! The noise was so loud the walls shook. Bart's flashlight flew from his hand and across the room. It lay in the middle of the floor, its feeble light aimed at the tutu box.

Bart didn't know whether to pick the flashlight up or leave it and run. After seconds, which seemed like hours, he moved toward the light and froze.

The tutu was sliding slowly out of the box. "Tony," Bart squeaked. "Is that you? Bob? Is this a joke?"

The only answer was a rustle of satin and tulle as the tutu began to rise, headless, armless, legless, and advance toward him.

He screamed and staggered backward, banging his leg on a chair. Then he whirled around, stumbling toward the stairs.

He fled up them, through the kitchen, up another flight, and down the hall. He flew into his bedroom, slammed and locked the door behind him, turned on one, two, all the lights, and, shaking, crawled into bed, face to the wall. I'm going crazy, he thought, panting. Then, no, I'm dreaming. That's it, I'm still asleep and I . . .

Squeak.

Cold enveloped the room. Oh my God, what was that?

Squeeeeeak.

Bart's blankets were sheets of ice. He didn't want to turn around, but he had to. He did it slowly, his eyes darting wildly around the room. Finally, they hit on the closet door. It was open about an inch. As he stared, it slid open an inch further.

No. Oh no! Wake up, Bart. Come on, wake up. He slapped at his face.

But the door continued to move. Soon it was open enough for him to see his dirty football uniform lying on the floor with the helmet on the shelf above. He watched in horror as the uniform began to straighten itself out and come toward him.

"No!" he yelled. "No!" He scrambled as far

back against the headboard of the bed as he could. But the uniform kept coming.

Click! Now what, he thought, and almost laughed hysterically at himself. His eyes flashed on his bedroom door.

Sure enough, it was opening. He saw a blaze of hot pink, and behind it streaks of electric blue, red, purple, and green. The tutus! They'd found him.

"Mom! Dad! Somebody help me!" he bellowed as the tutus and the uniform reached him. The lights went out. His arms and legs flailed. Perfume and sweat clogged his nostrils. He was being smothered by yards and yards of cloth. He gasped for breath.

Suddenly, a voice rang out. "Oh, for goodness' sake, Stryker, leave him alone."

Bart gasped again, but he felt the tutus, the uniform slide away. Panting and shivering, he lay with his eyes shut. The room was silent now, but still cold. Slowly he opened his eyes.

The lights were still out. The room was dark, except for a faint glow at the foot of his bed. It's not over, something in his brain whispered. Not yet.

He was right. The glow brightened, pulsing silver. It gathered, a roiling, shifting shape.

Terrified, Bart moaned. He couldn't move — he could only watch — as the glow trembled, wiggled, rounded. A form began to emerge — the form of a tall, slim, and rather pretty teenage girl in a long, old-fashioned dress with a ribbon in her hair. She smiled at him apologetically and said in a silvery voice, "I'm sorry about all this, Bart. Truly sorry."

He stared at her, blinked, and stared again. And then he thought, Well, Hawkins, it looks like 1351 Hexum is haunted after all.

Chapter 9

"I wouldn't have appeared to you if we didn't need your help so badly. But the situation has become impossible. We tried reasoning with Stryker, but that didn't work. We've also tried covering up his tracks — but he's very wily, and besides, not everything is reparable. Although occasionally he'll go away if we tell him to, we don't have the power to stop him outright. So you see, Bart, we really do need your help."

Bart was sitting up in bed, staring at the figure perched lightly on the chair at his desk. She looked quite real except for the fact that she was the color of starlight, and transparent to boot. "You . . . you know my name," he choked out.

"Yes. Yes, I do." She smiled. "Bartholomew Hawkins. But you don't like to be called that, do you? So it's Bart, Hawkins, or the Hawk. I know how you feel. I don't like my name much either, but Mother never allowed nicknames in — "

"Bu-but you're a ghost," Bart blurted out, cutting her off.

She didn't seem to mind. "Yes. I am," she said politely.

"You . . . you want to kill me!"

Then she did get upset. "Oh no, Bart. My goodness, no. Why would I want to do that?"

"You just tried to."

"Oh dear. I see I haven't been explaining myself properly. Mother always used to complain about that. 'Now, Millicent, from the beginning, pu-leeze,' she'd always say." The ghost laughed a silvery laugh.

Millicent. Bart found his tense muscles beginning to relax. A ghost named Millicent who laughed like that couldn't really want to kill him after all, could she? Then his hand brushed against the satin of one of the fallen tutus, and he shuddered again.

But Millicent, still smiling, said, "All right, for you — and Mother — I'll begin at the beginning." She gave a delicate cough, which made her waver and ripple. "This is a nice house. A very nice house. I really liked living in it when I was alive. I hoped to live a long time, but 1918 was a bad year for a lot of people, myself included. The war, the influenza. It was the latter that got me." She laughed again.

But Bart didn't find anything funny in her words. "The influenza? Do you mean the flu?"

"Yes. That's right. That *is* what you call it."

"You died of the *flu*?"

"Yes. A lot of people did back then. Don't

feel too bad. I had a fairly pleasant fourteen years up till then, so you can imagine my surprise when after I 'passed on,' I found myself still here, in this house, as a ghost. I always believed that ghosts were people who'd once had sad lives — or violent deaths. Well, neither was true in my case. Yet here I am — a spirit from the 'other side.' And I've been one for nearly seventy years."

"What!" exclaimed Bart. "You mean you were here when we moved in?"

"Certainly. I watched you almost trip over the doorjamb when you were helping your father with that heavy sofa. I wanted to offer a little assistance, but I thought it wouldn't be appreciated."

"But . . . but how come it's taken two years to find out I live in a haunted house?" Bart blurted out. He wondered briefly if he should have put that more politely. But, heck, how much experience do I have talking with ghosts, he asked himself.

In any case, Millicent took no offense. "That's what I was trying to tell you before," she said eagerly. "It's Stryker."

"Stryker? Who — or what — is he?"

"He's the poltergeist who's been making your — and your family's — life miserable for the past week. The one who threw your books around, broke the jam jars, wreaked havoc in the medicine cabinet, wrecked your brother's mobile, and nearly smothered you with the tutus. Not that even he'd go so far as to actually suffocate you; Stryker's thoroughly awful, but he isn't really evil. He moved into this house three weeks ago, and that's twenty-one days too long. He has to go — before it's too late."

By now completely caught up in Millicent's tale, Bart asked, "Too late for what?"

Millicent leaned forward. "Bart, what do you think will happen once your parents realize — which they most assuredly will — that all of the weird things happening in this house aren't being caused by a cat or a draft or an earthquake, but by one very obnoxious and persistent poltergeist?"

He thought a moment. "Well, the problem's never come up before, but I guess they'll call in someone who . . . um . . . specializes in getting rid of them, like the . . . uh . . . ghostbusters."

"Right. And what do you think will happen when these ghostbusters come in?"

"Uh . . . what?"

"We'll all have to go."

Bart was confused. "We? You mean me and my family? Why?"

"Oh dear, I *am* bad at explaining things. No, Bart, not you or your family. Me and my family, as it were."

"Your family?"

"Yes. Stryker and I are not the only ghosts in this house. There are a few others."

Bart felt a chill creep up his spine again. "A few others? How many is a few?"

"Let's see," Millicent said, concentrating. "There's Grace, Roderick, and Matthias —

72

Matthias is the one who fixed your brother's mobile. He's very handy — he used to build dollhouses as a hobby — Blaine and Duane the twins — they arrived after I did — Lurlene — she came from Mississippi originally — Lydia, and, of course, Old Man Koral. Did I forget anyone?"

"What about the beagle?" Bart asked, his voice rising hysterically.

"The beagle? I don't know of any beagle." Millicent sounded puzzled. "No, that's everyone. Nine of us in all — plus Stryker."

"Oh my God," Bart moaned, burying his face in his hands.

"Rather than have all nine of us appear to you at once . . ."

"Oh my God," Bart whimpered again.

"We took a vote and I won. I'm the official spokesperson. Or perhaps I should say spokespook." She laughed, but this time it didn't have the desired effect on Bart. He still had his face in his hands. "I guess it *is* a bit of a shock finding out there are ten ghosts in your house." She stopped speaking to give him a chance to recover.

He did and, picking his head up, he stared hard at her for a full thirty seconds, which was difficult because she shimmered and shifted in his chair. At last he said, "Just what do you expect me to do?"

It seemed to him that her eyes were brighter. "Get rid of Stryker before your family does."

"And just how am I supposed to do that?"

"I . . . I'm not sure," she faltered. "But you're smart and sensitive and you know more about ghosts than anyone else in your family. After all, you've read *The Haunting of Hill House*."

Bart didn't bother to ask how she knew that — or various other things about him. Instead, he said, "Why should I help you?"

"That's a reasonable question," said Millicent. "The answer is we love this place. It's our home too. We've been here for years, decades, some of us even centuries. We don't want to leave. That's why we're begging you to help us stay. And then it will be just as it was before — none of us will ever bother you again. You'll never know we're here."

Bart kept looking at her. Her tone was compelling and she seemed an okay sort — for a ghost. But then he shook his head. "No, I can't. I wouldn't know what to do."

Millicent shifted again, and it seemed to Bart her voice took on a hard edge. "All right, what do you want?"

"Want?" Bart asked, puzzled. "What do you mean?"

"What are you asking for in exchange for your help?"

"You mean like a reward?"

"Yes. Lurlene said I'd probably have to bargain with you, so go ahead. Name your price."

Bart was still surprised by her new approach. Then he remembered something about Old Man

74

Koral and a buried treasure. Was that what she was offering him? He asked her.

"A treasure? I think Old Man Koral once buried some coins. But I don't think they're worth much. Fifty dollars or so. There is a lovely garnet necklace Grace lost under a floorboard in Leanne's room. That's probably worth a few hundred dollars. So, if that'll do . . ."

"No," Bart said. "It won't."

"You don't think it's enough money?" Millicent said coldly.

"No, I mean, I don't want money."

"Well, what do you want?"

Bart was silent. An idea was forming in his head. A disturbing idea. What do you want, Millicent had asked. I want the Phantoms to win the league championship, he'd thought automatically. There was a good chance his team would do that. But there was also the possibility of another team, say the Surgeons, winning, especially if it came down to a play-off between those two teams. But just suppose Millicent and her pals could offer a little ghostly intervention? Just suppose . . . no. Bart shook his head. That would be cheating. He closed his eyes and saw the two teams battling it out, thirty seconds to go and the Phantoms ahead by three points. Then he saw the Surgeons' fullback running for the end zone. He was going to make it. . . .

"No!" Bart yelled.

"All right. You don't have to shout," said

Millicent. "I thought you'd be willing to help us. I guess I was . . ."

"How are you and your friends at — football?" Bart interrupted her.

"Football?" Millicent said in a puzzled voice. "I don't know."

"Could you find out?"

"Sure. I'll be right back." In a flash she was gone.

She'll say they're rotten, Bart thought, half wishing it were true and half wishing it weren't. He waited restlessly, not knowing what to do with his conscience.

In a few moments, Millicent returned. "Except for Lurlene, with a little practice we're first class. We can beat any team in North America, past or present, except maybe the 1967 Green Bay Packers."

Bart swallowed hard. It took him almost a full minute to say, "Well then, Millie. I think you just might have yourself a deal."

Chapter 10

"Ah!" Bart yelled. His eyes snapped open and his hand flew to the top of his head. He heaved a sigh of relief, as thick waves of hair rippled under his hand. That dream again. Why did he have it so often? Why did he have it at all? There've gotta be worse things to worry about than going bald, he thought, like . . . Oh no! Suddenly, all of the preceding night came flooding back to him. The party, the broken lamp, the ripped tutu, the . . . the . . . "Ghosts!" he exclaimed. "We've got ten ghosts, and I made a deal with one of them!" He slapped the side of his head with his hand. "The phantoms will make sure the Phantoms win the league championship and what do I have to do in return? Move a mountain? No. Pilot a spaceship to Pluto? No. Become president of the United States? No. All I have to do is rid this house of one crummy little poltergeist. That's all." He slapped the side of his head again. "I must be nuts. Totally, completely nuts." He sank back onto the bed and pulled a pillow over his face.

In the hallway, the phone began to ring. "Ohhh," Bart groaned. He tossed the pillow away, crawled out of his tangle of blankets, and went to answer it.

"Hello," he said. "Hawkins residence?"

"I think that's supposed to be my question," a woman's voice replied with a chuckle.

"Who is this? I mean, who's calling, please?" He'd been trained by his mother since age six in the proper way to take a message. It's a good thing it wasn't her on the line, he thought.

"This is Eleanor Nutley. Your mother wanted some information on opera tickets," the woman answered.

Bart vaguely remembered his mother saying something about that. He got out a pen and scribbled the dates and times and prices Eleanor Nutley was throwing at him.

"And on November nineteenth, they're doing *Macbeth*."

"*Macbeth!*" Bart blurted out. "I thought you said these were opera tickets." Darn it, he swore at himself.

Mrs. Nutley sounded amused. "Yes, they are. *Macbeth* is an opera as well as a play."

"Oh," he mumbled. "I didn't know that."

"Do you like Shakespeare, Bart? This is Bart, isn't it?"

"Yes. I mean, no. I mean. Yes, this is Bart. But . . . uh . . . no, I don't care about . . . uh . . . Shakespeare," he lied.

"Oh, that's too bad."

In response, Bart said, "Let me see if I got all these times down correctly, Mrs. Nutley." He read the opera ticket list back to her.

"Perfect. Thank you, Bart."

"You're welcome, Mrs. Nutley." He hung up. "Whew," he said. But no sooner did he take his hand off the cordless receiver than the phone rang again. "Hello, Hawkins residence," he said with what he thought was crispness.

"What's wrong?" a familiar voice demanded.

"Oh hi, Mom. Nothing's wrong."

"But you sound tense."

"I'm fine, Mom." He tried to make his voice easier. I'll tell her about the lamp and the tutu later when I've made up a good enough lie, he thought. "How's Grandma?"

"She's having a serious attack of the vapors," Mrs. Hawkins said.

Bart chuckled. "The vapors" was his mother's expression for Grandma's nerves.

"Yes, well, don't make fun of her," she said, without admitting that she'd just done that herself. "She's very sensitive." She paused a moment, then said, "She asked if we could stay another day. I told her I'd check with you and Leanne."

"It's fine with me," Bart said. Very fine, he added silently. "Leanne's not back yet, but I bet it's okay with her too."

"Yes, it is. I called her at Rocky's Aunt Peggy's. She said she'd come back later to check up . . . I mean, to keep you company."

"She doesn't have to. I've got all the company I need," he said. Like ten ghosts to be exact, he thought.

"You do? Who's with you?"

"No one right now." That I can see. "But they'll be here later. Don't worry, Mom." I'll worry enough for both of us, he added silently.

"Well, all right. . . . How was the dance last night? Did you have a good time?"

"Very good."

"Was your costume a hit?"

"Yes," he said with a genuine smile.

"Good. Well, I don't want to tie up Grandma and Grandpa's line. We'll see you tomorrow. Call us if there's any problem."

"I will, Mom." I won't, Mom. He hung up.

Then he went into the bathroom to shower. He'd just stepped out, dripping, when the phone rang a third time. "Sheesh," he said, wrapping a towel around his waist and squishing into the hall. This time he was careful to intone "Hello. Hawkins residence" firmly and calmly as he carried the cordless receiver into his bedroom.

"You're not still angry, are you?" Lisa's voice asked.

"What? Oh. No. Not really. It was my own fault." With the receiver tucked under his chin, he started to pull on his sweatpants.

"Your fault? How?"

"For having the party. For letting them bring beer."

"But it was a good party," Lisa said, surprised. "And everybody drinks beer. You couldn't tell them not to bring it. You'd be a . . ."

"Nerd," Bart finished for her.

"Well, not exactly. You could never be a nerd. You know that."

"Right. I know that. The Hawk doesn't have a trace of nerddom in his manly body. He could even read Shakespeare and not win the Wimp of the Year Award," he said sarcastically.

"What?" Lisa was obviously confused by his tone.

"Nothing, my queen," he said lightly.

She didn't respond for a moment. Then she asked, "What are you going to tell your parents?"

It was a good question — one he'd been thinking about in the shower.

The lamp was easy. He'd say he'd bumped into it while he was doing his jumping jacks. Not a very good lie; however, his parents would accept it because he was taking the blame. But the tutu. That was harder. He couldn't very well say he'd suddenly had the urge to become a ballet dancer instead of a football player. He glanced over at the floor. His brow puckered. The tutus weren't there. Then he noticed that they were lying in a neat pile on his chair.

"I could come over and fix that costume for you now before they come back," Lisa offered.

"Hmmm." The phone still under his chin, Bart crossed to the chair and sifted through the pile of tutus until he found the hot-pink one.

He pulled it out and examined it. His eyes widened. "No," he said slowly, "you don't have to."

"But I want to . . ."

"You don't have to because I . . . uh . . . fixed it myself."

"*You* did?"

"Sure. Can't Bart the non-nerd sew?"

There was another pause. Then Lisa said, "You're in a weird mood."

Bart didn't respond. He was still looking at the tutu. The place where it had been ripped was now neatly sewn with stitches so fine you practically needed a magnifying glass to see them. He ran his finger over them. They were so delicately done he could barely feel them.

"Well, anyway. You don't have to hang around until your folks get home, do you? I thought we could have a picnic today. I'll make the sandwiches. . . ."

When Bart still didn't answer, Lisa said, "Bart, are you there?"

"Uh . . . yeah. Sure. What did you say?"

"A picnic, Bart. P-I-C-N-I-C. Do — you — want — to — go?"

"Yeah. Sounds good. But I've got some . . . things to take care of first."

"What things?"

"Oh, you know. I've got to work out and stuff."

"How long do you think it'll take?"

"A while. I'll call you when I'm done."

"Bart. Is something else wrong?" Lisa asked.

"Not yet. . . . I mean, not now." Then, in a lower voice, he said, "Don't put any onions on the sandwiches, baby."

"I won't. Especially since they're peanut butter and jelly," Lisa answered dryly and hung up.

Bart put down the phone and folded the tutu on top of the others. He threw on his sweatshirt, lifted up the pile of costumes, carried it downstairs, and placed it in the box in the rec room. As he began his daily push-ups, he said, "Okay, Millicent. You've proved you can sew. But as for playing football, that remains to be seen. In the meantime, I guess I owe you one. So, in about an hour, I, Bart Hawkins, am going to risk my reputation and my love life for you and your pals. I am going to spend the whole morning in the public library."

Chapter 11

"To get rid of a ghost, boil up three prickly pear roots in stump water and sprinkle your yard with the water." Now that's real useful, Bart thought. He was bent over a fat reference book called the *Encyclopedia of Ghosts and Apparitions*. It was the fourth book he'd looked at that morning, and, so far, it wasn't proving any more helpful than the first three.

But he read on, "If your house is haunted, take rosemary, horn, and cow dung. Mix them together. Burn the mixture and the ghost will depart." Great. Mom would really love the smell of cow dung around the house, he thought. He scanned the page. Hmmm, how about this one: "To clear a house of ghosts, get a pair of brass cymbals. Strike them together nine times, each time repeating, 'Avaunt, ye ancestral manes!'" Ye ancestral manes? Bart stifled a laugh. It sounded like a pack of dead lions. Then he sighed again and rubbed his forehead. Finding a practical method of exorcising a poltergeist was turning out to be even harder than he'd imagined. First of all, whatever method he used had to be something his parents and siblings wouldn't notice. That was hard because a lot of the techniques, such as burning cow dung, were *very* noticeable — even if he were able to do them when all his family was out of the house. But second, and even more of a problem, was the fact that everything he came across told him how to get rid of ghosts, plural. What could he do to eliminate one ghost, but not drive all the others away?

Bart did a slow neck roll to unkink his muscles. Then he looked up at the clock. One-fifteen, it said. Jeez, I've been here nearly three hours, and I haven't even had lunch. In immediate response, his stomach started grumbling. He patted it. Another half hour, that's all, he told it. It answered with a louder growl. All right, fifteen minutes. His stomach murmured something back. Bart patted it again and returned to the book. "If you're troubled by ghosts, sprinkle quicksilver on the floor." No. "Shouting 'Ram, ram' drives away all ghosts." No, no. *Grr* went his guts. Okay, okay. Bart gave in. He was about to close the book when something caught his eye. "Ghosts can be banished betwixt the door and the doorpost. If you slam the door, they will leave in a hurry." Hmmm. He read it over again. "Ghosts can be banished betwixt the door and the doorpost. . . ." Does that mean if you catch a ghost as it's entering or leaving your room and slam the door on it, you can get rid of it? Hmmm. He picked up his pen and wrote the two sentences down on a small notepad and pocketed the pad. Feeling that perhaps the morning wasn't a total loss after all, he shut the book and returned it to the librarian. He left the library, congratulating himself on finding something that might solve his problem and on not being seen there by anybody who mattered, when a pile of books with legs bumped into him. The books crashed to the ground, revealing none other than Arvie Biedemeyer.

Arvie clucked his tongue. "I hope none of the spines are broken," he said. He frowned up at the accused spine-breaker and his expression changed. "Oh, hello, Bart." His voice was friendly. "Do you come to the library often? I've never seen you here before."

"Hi, Arvie," Bart answered. What's with this guy? I hardly ran into him at all before. Now he's worse than a wad of chewing gum stuck to the bottom of my sneaker. "No. I never come here. I was . . . uh . . . doing a favor for my sister. Returning some books."

"Oh," said Arvie. He stooped down to gather his books. "How's your ankle?"

"Fine," Bart answered, bending to help him.

"That's good. And your voice projection practice?"

"My what? Oh. Oh, right. It's . . . uh . . . coming along." He spotted a red-covered book that had bounced into the dirt under a tree.

"You know, I regretted being the cause of

your injury, but I rather enjoyed conversing with you the other day." Arvie reached for a book, lost his balance, and plopped down on his rear end. "I realize the feeling probably wasn't mutual," he continued after getting back on his feet with a small grunt. "But — "

"Arvie," Bart interrupted. "Are you returning this?" He held up the book he'd retrieved. The title was *Poltergeists Explained.*

Arvie squinted at it. "That? Yes. It's not bad for what it is — although I've read better. There's a pretty good section describing the theory that poltergeists often manifest in houses where there are troubled children or adolescents. A nice blending of the psychological and parapsychological . . ." Abruptly, Arvie stopped. "Are you interested in poltergeists?" he asked bluntly.

"Who me? Nah," Bart answered quickly. "But my, uh, sister loves 'em. I mean, she loves reading about them. Maybe I'll take this book out for her."

"You're very considerate of your sister," Arvie said.

Bart gave him a sharp look, but he quickly realized that Arvie wasn't being sarcastic. In fact, if anything, he seemed pleased at the idea. "I . . . uh . . . guess so," Bart answered.

"Leanne."

"Huh?"

"That's your sister's name, isn't it?"

"Yeah," Bart answered, a feeling of dread creeping up into his throat. "You know her?"

"Only by sight," Arvie said. "Her band played at the dance last night in Folger."

Bart's dread was replaced by a different feeling entirely. "You went to that dance?" he asked in astonishment. "How come? You don't usually go to the dances at DeForest, do you?"

"No. But my cousin lives in Folger. She needed a date. Your sister, Leanne — she has a great voice," Arvie said, and promptly turned beet red.

Bart's astonishment changed to a mixture of amusement and pity. Holy cow dung, he thought. The guy's got a king-sized, grade-A crush on old Donuthead. He fought down the urge to laugh. "Yeah? I mean, yeah, I guess she does. I'll tell her you said so."

"No," Arvie said quickly. "Don't do that."

Bart looked at him strangely and shrugged. "Okay.... Uh, Arvie, I've got to go. If you could return this book so I can take it out for Leanne, I'd appreciate it."

"Oh, right," Arvie said. Still red-faced, he turned toward the library. Shaking his head, Bart followed him.

Chapter 12

Poltergeists Explained was fascinating. Useless, but fascinating. It gave all the cases, theories, data Bart cared to read about the noisy ghosts. What it *didn't* tell was how to get rid of them. Oh, there were accounts of poltergeists who left after being ordered to go by clergymen or professional ghost hunters, but Bart's job was to prevent the pros from being called in. One encouraging thing in the book, though, was the fact that most poltergeists don't haunt a house for very long. A month, the author said, is the average, although some stick around for as long as six months. Then there are the few who never leave at all. Bart hoped fervently that Stryker was not one of those.

He put down the book and yawned. I think I need a little fresh air, he thought. I've been reading for hours and . . . oh no! He slapped his cheek. Lisa! I've forgotten all about her and the picnic. He picked up the phone that was still lying on his desk and dialed her number. Her line rang seven times before someone picked it up and said hello. It was Lisa's younger sister, Jacey. The two sisters were very close.

"Jacey, let me speak to Lisa," he said.

"Who is this?" Jacey asked.

Bart rolled his eyes. "Who do you think it is? Godzilla?"

"Too bad, Godzilla. Lisa doesn't talk to monsters," she answered snidely.

"Come on, Jacey. It's Bart, and just put Lisa on, will you?"

"I'll see if she's interested in talking to you, Mr. Hawkins."

"Mr. Hawkins. Jeez," Bart said as he waited for Lisa to come to the phone. Okay, so I forgot, he thought. And she's mad at me, so Jacey's mad at me too. But there's still plenty of time for a picnic, so she can't stay mad at me for too long, can she?

"Hello, Lisa Bonnard speaking."

"Look, Lisa, I'm sorry. . . . I . . . uh . . . got involved in a . . . project, and I lost track of the time. But I'm finished now, and I could sure go for a peanut butter and jelly sandwich."

"Who is this, please?"

"Oh for pete's sake, it's Bart, short for Bartholomew Richard Hawkins."

There was a long silence on the other end. Then Lisa choked. "Bartholomew," she said, and began to giggle.

Bart felt heat rise to his cheeks. Why on earth did I tell her that, he moaned to himself. I've kept that name from everybody. "It's a family name," he said stiffly.

But Lisa kept giggling.

"Jeez, it's not *that* funny a word!" he snapped, exasperated.

"I'm sorry. I can't . . . help it. It sounds like a name for a . . . kitten. Bartholo*mew*." She made the last syllable sound like a baby cat asking its mother for food.

It was Bart's turn to be silent.

Lisa finally stopped laughing and apologized. "I'm sorry. I didn't mean to make fun of you, Bart. I promise I won't tell anyone else what your real name is." Another short giggle escaped her.

Bart didn't say anything. He'd be darned if he forgave her that easily, or worse yet made her swear to keep that promise.

"Can you come over now?" she went on. "The sandwiches are all ready. They've been ready for hours." She said the last sentence a bit tightly, as though she'd just remembered that she was supposed to be angry with him.

Bart waited a few moments more, then said coolly, "Yeah. All right. See you soon." He put down the phone. Sometimes, Hawkins, you're not too bright, he told himself. He straightened up his room, hiding the poltergeist book and his notepad and replacing the phone in the hall. Then he wrote a note for Leanne. "Dear Donuthead," he began. Realizing he'd do better with "sugar than vinegar," as Grandma Hawkins liked to say, he crumpled it and began a new note:

> Dear Leanne,
>   Mom told me you'd be checking in, so this is to let you know everything's okay. I'm going out with Lisa and won't be back until tonight. If you want to stay over at Rocky's or somebody else's, that's cool.
> Bart.
> P.S. I heard from your secret admirer that you sang great last night.

He read the note over once, pinned it to the bulletin board in the kitchen, and left the house.

The picnic wasn't a great success, at least for Bart. He was distracted, thinking about all the stuff he'd read that morning. But he didn't think Lisa really noticed. At about five-thirty, when it started to get dark, he got hungry again and offered to treat Lisa to dinner at Yumby's. Afterward, they went roller skating. Greg, Kristi, and some of the other kids were at the rink. Bob and Tony weren't, which Bart thought was just as well.

By nine he was ready to call it a night, but then he had to go to Yumby's again with the crowd. So it wasn't until ten-thirty that he finally got home. He slouched into the kitchen and saw that his note had been replaced by one of Leanne's:

Dear Bart,

Glad to know all is well. I'm spending the night at Carol's, but I'll be home before Mom and Dad get back.

Leanne.

P.S. I didn't know you know anyone who goes to Folger High.

Bart smiled at the last sentence. Leanne wouldn't come out and ask point-blank who her secret admirer was, and he knew it, which was why at the same time he could both tease her and keep his promise to Arvie not to reveal his identity. He threw away the note, poured and drank a large glass of milk, and went upstairs.

He'd just slipped into his pajamas and shut the light when the air near his desk started to shimmer. Oh no, he thought, tensing. Stryker. But then he realized there was no sensation of cold, and that the poltergeist had never shimmered before. His muscles relaxed, and he found himself smiling as Millicent appeared.

"Hello, Millicent," he said.

"Hello, Bart. Please call me Millie. I liked when you did before."

"Okay, Millie," he said, still smiling.

"Well, I see you're alone again tonight."

"Yes. My folks won't be back until tomorrow."

"Did you have a good day?"

"It was okay. I did some research about poltergeists. I went on a picnic with my girlfriend.

Then we went out to dinner and roller skating. I'm pretty tired now."

"I had an interesting day too. I found a secret compartment. Eighty-four years in this house and it still has a few surprises. Actually, I shouldn't say that *I* found the compartment. Lydia told me about it, after Old Man Koral remembered and told her."

"A secret compartment? Where is it?" Bart perked up.

"Up in the Lilac Room."

"The Lilac Room? Oh, you mean the room that was boarded up." He recalled peeling wallpaper with purple flowers on it before they'd painted. Now the room was used for storage. "What was in it?" He asked, feeling excitement rising in him.

"A bed, a chair, a vanity. The usual, really. It was Lurlene's boudoir. She was killed there by her jealous husband. That's why it was boarded . . ."

"Not the room. The compartment. What was in the secret compartment?" Bart cut in.

"Oh. Nothing."

"Nothing?" Bart's excitement sank.

"No, but you could put something in it. Would you like me to show it to you?"

"Some other time maybe." He yawned.

"Don't you like to explore this house? I did. I still do."

"I explored it plenty when we first moved in." He yawned again.

"That's right. You did," Millicent said with a faint smile.

Suddenly, Bart felt uncomfortable. "You've watched me a lot, haven't you?" he said.

"Yes," Millicent answered simply. "There hasn't been anybody close to my age in this house since my distant cousin Polly lived here in 1947."

There was no sadness or self-pity in Millicent's voice, but Bart felt a tug at his heart. Forty years was a long time to be without a friend, even if you were a ghost. After a moment, he said, "I . . . uh . . . almost forgot. I want to . . . um . . . thank you for fixing the tutu. You must've been, I mean, you must be real good at sewing."

"Yes, I am. Needlepoint and embroidery too. The so-called 'feminine arts.' It's a wonder I am any good at them. I was terrible at everything else a girl was supposed to be able to do."

Bart cupped his chin in his hand. "What else was a girl supposed to be able to do back then?"

"Cooking and cleaning, of course. Gardening. Flower arranging. Singing, dancing, playing the piano, and making polite conversation."

"You seem pretty good at polite conversation to me."

Millicent laughed.

"What other things were you good at?" Bart wasn't feeling so tired anymore. He was getting too interested in this ghost to be tired.

"Climbing trees. Walking fences. Winning at

95

marbles. And getting into trouble. When I was ten, you know what I wanted to be more than anything in the world?" she asked.

"What?"

"A movie star. Isn't that crazy?"

"It doesn't sound so crazy to me. A lot of kids want to be that."

"But not in 1914, when you came from a 'good family.' And especially not if the movie star you wanted to be was Pearl White."

"Who?"

"Pearl White. You've never heard of her? She was so famous then, but fame's funny. Here today, gone tomorrow. That's one of my father's phrases."

"My dad uses it too. I knew it was old and corny, but not *that* old and corny."

"I suspect it's even older and cornier than both of us can imagine. Anyway, Pearl White was the star of a movie serial called *The Perils of Pauline*. Each week she got into another thrilling adventure, drifting away in a hot air balloon, being blown up at sea by pirates, getting kidnapped by masked outlaws. Then, at the end of each episode, she was rescued by her manly suitor, Harry."

Talk about old and corny, he thought.

But then Millicent went on. "I thought Harry was a jerk and the stories kind of silly. But I also knew that Pearl White did those crazy daredevil feats and that's what was really exciting. That's what *I* wanted to do."

Bart looked at the silvery ghost in the dainty

dress in astonishment. "A stuntwoman? You wanted to be a stuntwoman?"

"Is that what it's called? That's a good word for it. Yes, I would have loved to have been a stuntwoman more than anything in the world. But I wouldn't have been. I'd have been a teacher or a shopkeeper or a homemaker. Here today, gone tomorrow."

Suddenly, Bart felt another tug. Not only had Millicent never become a stuntwoman, but she'd never become anything else either — except a ghost.

She must've sensed his mood, because she smiled and said, "Well, tell me about your poltergeist research so I can report to the others."

Bart gave himself a little shake. "Oh. Right. The others. Well, I read a lot of books. They were interesting, but they didn't tell me much about getting rid of poltergeists. Except for this idea . . ." He told her about catching the poltergeist between door and doorpost and slamming the door. "What do you think? Will it work?"

"I don't know. I may be a ghost, but I don't know how to get rid of one. I suppose it's worth a try though — if you can catch Stryker in that position."

"Well, that's not very encouraging."

"Sorry. But you see that's why we need your help."

Bart frowned. Then he said, "I also found out that most poltergeists don't stick around long.

Maybe if Stryker knows I'm onto him, he'll leave."

"It's possible, but I wouldn't bet on it," said Millicent.

"Great! You're going to stand . . . uh . . . float there and tell me how nothing I've come up with is going to work," Bart said.

Millicent gave a ghostly little shrug. "I told you I'm not very good at polite conversation."

"It isn't polite conversation I need. It's brilliant ideas."

"I'm not good at brilliant ideas either. But I have faith in you, Bart. We all do. You'll come up with something. We know you will."

"Listen, Millie. When I said I'd help, I didn't think that . . ."

"We've been practicing football, Bart," she interrupted. "We're getting quite good."

"You're what? You are? How . . ."

"Yes. You'll see." Before he could say anything else, she said, "Now I'd better let you go to sleep. You've had a busy day." She faded out of sight.

Bart stared at the place she'd been and shook his head. Then he yawned. Sliding under the covers, he wondered if winning the league championship was going to be ample payment for this job.

Chapter 13

The weather was still balmy, but Bart was spending Sunday morning much like the day before — reading. The public library was closed, so he'd decided to go through the Hawkinses' own library, in hopes of coming across some other useful information on ghosts.

It was tough going — but interesting all the same. He had to leaf through novels and short story collections to find ones about ghosts. Some of the stories he read on the spot. The novels he laid aside to read later.

Lisa was visiting relatives, which was just as well, but Greg and Tom Brewster called asking him to join them for various activities. He put them off. Tony called too to apologize. "Uh . . . about the other night. I'm sorry. I hope your folks didn't give you a rough time."

"Nah," Bart said, not bothering to tell him he hadn't told his parents yet.

"That's good. My folks did."

"Yeah?"

"Yeah. They told me if they catch me drunk

ever again, they'll ground me for the year."

Personally, Bart was beginning to believe that maybe Tony's parents were right, but he commiserated with him and got off the phone as fast as he could.

After four hours of research, he still hadn't found out much more about eliminating ghosts, and he was definitely feeling the need for some sun and exercise, so he got out his bike and rode to Rowan Woods.

He got to the woods in record time, parked his bike, and decided to explore the old log cabin. It looked much the same as it had before, except maybe dustier, but this time, while Bart was running his hand over the fireplace, he noticed a brass button in the center of a carved wooden flower. He pushed it and out of the bottom of the mantelpiece a small drawer appeared. "A secret compartment!" he exclaimed. Excitedly, he bent down and looked inside. There was nothing there but some yellowing papers. He removed and unfolded them carefully. Written on them in scratchy ink were drawings of something that looked like a box with coils and wires in it. Beneath the drawings were notes he couldn't decipher and mathematical formulas he couldn't follow. I wonder if Arvie knows about these, Bart thought. He refolded the papers and put them back. Jeez, the second secret compartment to turn up in two days and both are busts, he thought. He pushed the drawer back into the mantelpiece and left the cabin. For an hour afterward he sat on a rock by the stream. Then he decided to return home.

He was wondering which novel he should read first when he saw his parents' car in the driveway. Dusty was leaning against it, reading another one of his mathematical puzzle magazines. So much for more research today, Bart thought. "Hi, Dusty," he said. "Have a good time at Grandma and Grandpa's?"

"What do you think?" Dusty grimaced. "Guess how many times Grandma said, 'Oh, my nerves' this time."

"How many?"

"Sixteen."

"Is that a record?"

"No. Last time it was seventeen, and we were there two hours less."

"Hmmm. Maybe she's getting better."

In answer, Dusty rolled his eyes.

"Mom and Dad inside?" Bart changed the topic.

"Yeah. I think they want to talk with you. Something about a lamp."

"Right," Bart said with a sigh. He walked into the house.

His parents were sitting in the living room. He greeted them with "I hear Grandma's feeling better."

"She is? I mean, yes, she is," Mrs. Hawkins said. "However, we can discuss Grandma later. Right now, I'd appreciate it if you'd tell us what happened to the lamp in the rec room."

"I was ... uh ... planning to," Bart answered

and went into the story he'd prepared.

When he finished, his father said, "You see, Maura. I knew there'd be a good explanation. Bart isn't the type of boy to have wild parties while his parents are away." He winked at his son.

Bart knew he was supposed to smile in response, so he did, but he almost had to lift the corners of his mouth with his fingers to do it.

"All right," said his mother. "But what about the dishes?"

"The dishes? What dishes?" Bart asked.

"There were two broken dishes in the sink."

"There were? I don't know anything about..." Bart began and then broke off. Stryker! Stryker was at it again. And Bart had to cover up for him fast. "Oh, the *dishes*," he said. "I . . . uh . . . put them in the dishrack to dry and that dumb cat Kingston came in through the kitchen window and knocked them into the sink."

"Well, why didn't you clean up the broken pieces?"

"Uh . . . that's a good question. Because . . . uh . . . the phone rang. It was . . . uh . . . Mrs. Nutley. That's right. I took down that information for you about the opera tickets. And then . . ."

Bart was interrupted by the sound of the front door opening, followed by his sister's appearance in the living room. "Hi, Mom. Hi, Dad. We really sounded great Friday night. You would've . . ."

"Leanne," Mrs. Hawkins cut her off. "We want to hear all about your concert — just as soon as Bart finishes explaining about the broken dishes in the kitchen sink."

"The broken dishes!" Leanne's hand flew to her mouth.

Mr. and Mrs. Hawkins didn't seem to notice her reaction, but Bart gave her a funny look.

"You may continue," his mother said to him.

"Well, so the cat broke them and then Mrs. Nutley called and right after she called, Greg called. By then, I'd . . . uh . . . forgotten about the dishes. I'm sorry. I'll clean them up now if you want."

"I've already done that." Mrs. Hawkins frowned. "It seems odd, though. We go away for two days and half the things in the house get broken."

"That's hyperbole, Maura," Mr. Hawkins teased, throwing one of his wife's favorite words back at her.

"I'm aware that it is, Howard," she said.

Bart stiffened. She doesn't believe me, he thought. There was an uncomfortable pause.

Then, Mrs. Hawkins said, "I'm going to have to talk to the Baxters about their cat."

Bart relaxed. He felt as though he'd just had a crate of dishes removed from his back. But only for a minute. Stryker had struck again — and he would go on striking. And that meant that Bart had better be around to cover up for him.

Bart spent the rest of the day anxiously

hovering around his parents and trying not to seem anxious. Lisa, who'd returned from her relatives, called to ask him to go skating, but he turned her down. Bob phoned and said he'd gotten a tape of Super Bowl highlights that Bart had been dying to see, but Bart told him he was needed at home.

I can't believe I'm doing this — spending all Sunday hanging around with my folks — he thought. If only I could go upstairs and read some of those novels. But he didn't want to let his parents out of his sight. In the back of his mind, he knew it might be awfully hard covering up for a poltergeist — especially if it decided to do something like fling the grandfather clock across the room or rearrange the sofa while they were sitting on it. But he couldn't think of anything to do to get rid of the ghost once and for all.

Finally, after dinner, his parents went for a walk, and Bart breathed a sigh of relief — until he realized that Leanne was still there.

"Aren't you going to rehearse or something? Dusty's practicing for the school math-off, or whatever it's called, at his friend Manny's house." Bart knew that sounded weird.

But Leanne didn't seem to notice. "Listen," she said. "I . . . uh . . . want to thank you. I mean, I don't know what you did it for, but thanks just the same. I promise to . . . uh . . . repay you."

Bart blinked at her. What on earth was she talking about? Then he remembered. The secret admirer. "Well, it just goes to show you some people have taste," he said.

Leanne looked at him blankly.

"Just because to me the Jazzettes sound like a slightly warped recording of the inside of the dog pound at feeding time doesn't mean everybody has . . ."

"What?" Leanne shouted, her face turning pale with anger. "The Jazzettes sound like what? You creep! I thank you for doing me a favor and then you . . . you . . ." All of a sudden, she stopped, looking confused. "I don't get it. Why *did* you do me a favor? Why'd you tell Mom the cat broke those dishes when you know I did?"

"*You? You* broke them? You mean it wasn't Stry — I mean, but you came home after I did."

"No, I came home earlier. I made myself lunch, and as I was washing the dishes, they slipped out of my hands and smashed in the sink. I meant to clean them up, but the phone rang. It was Rocky. She wrote a new tune. I just had to go hear it and I forgot about the dishes. I thought it was real clever how you guessed that I'd been interrupted by a phone call and you used that excuse yourself."

"Very clever," Bart muttered.

"But I still don't get it. Why did you cover up for me?"

Bart let out a snicker and, thinking it was too bad that pun-loving Greg wouldn't get to hear this one, said, "Let's just say it's because I was in good *spirits*."

Chapter 14

"I'm telling you, Millie. It's been nearly a week. I haven't seen him and you haven't seen him, so he must be gone." Bart was sitting up in bed. He'd finally finished reading *Macbeth*, and he was glad to have the ghost's company; the play had given him the creeps.

Actually, he'd had a lot of Millicent's company that week. She told him many stories of her life in the early 1900s — and in other decades too, which she'd seen through ghostly eyes. Bart in turn talked about football, films, music, and especially books. He learned that Millicent had read some of the same ones he had. She recommended some books to him, too. He was delighted. Here was someone who didn't seem to think he was a jerk or a genius for wanting to read!

"I hope so, Bart. I really hope so," Millicent replied. "But I feel in my bones he's not."

"You don't have any bones."

"You know what I mean."

"Well, I feel in *my* bones he is — and it's a darn good thing, too. My friends are beginning to wonder how come I rush home from school after practice every day instead of hanging out with them at Yumby's."

"Why do you rush home every day?"

Bart gave the ghost an "Are you kidding me?" look. "To try to cover up for anything Stryker might do. Why else?"

"But he might do all sorts of things while you're in school. Then what will you do?"

Bart sighed. That problem had crossed his mind, and he didn't have any solution to it. "I don't know," he finally said. "Actually, I've been hoping he'd show up in my room so I could try that 'betwixt door and doorpost' business on him. But now that he's gone, it doesn't matter anyway. The point, as Mr. Moffatt, my history teacher would say, is 'moot.' "

After a pause, Millicent changed the subject. "Tell me about your friends."

"My friends? Why?"

"I'm curious. I was a curious girl and now I'm a curious ghost."

"Well, my best friend is a guy named Greg. You've probably seen him. He's been here a lot. He's tall and thin. You wouldn't think he's much of an athlete to look at him, but he's a great end. He catches passes well and he runs fast. He's really funny, too, always making bad puns. You'd probably like him."

"Yes, I have seen him. And I do like him."

"Great. He'd probably like you too," Bart

said. "I mean, if he could meet you. Then there're Bob and Tony. They're okay guys, basically. A little thoughtless and dumb, but okay. There's also Tom Brewster — he comes over sometimes — the rest of the guys on the team, and other kids from school. I know most of them. I guess you could say I'm pretty popular."

"What about your girlfriend? You haven't mentioned her."

"Lisa?" he said with surprise. "I guess I haven't, but I thought you meant just my friends."

"I didn't know a girlfriend couldn't be a friend," Millicent teased. "Anyway, tell me about her."

"Well, you must've seen *her* here. She's blond, blue-eyed, very pretty. She's popular too — captain of the cheerleading squad, vice president of the junior class. She's always trying to help people. She's fun to be with and she's got a great . . ." He stopped.

"A great what?"

"Body," he mumbled.

"Why are you embarrassed? She does have a lovely figure, much better than mine was. I looked like an ironing board."

"No, you don't," Bart said, trying to focus on her shimmering form. "You're tall and slender. You'd probably have made a good model."

"An artist's model? For people to draw?"

"No, a fashion model. For people to photograph and put in magazines."

"How dull!" Millicent said.

"Some girls would give anything to do that."

"How peculiar."

Bart laughed.

Then Millicent said, "Do you love Lisa?"

He gave her a funny look. "Well, yeah. Sure. She's my girlfriend, isn't she?" he finally said. Then, "Why? Why'd you ask me that?"

"Because you don't always seem to be . . ." She paused. "On the same wavelength with her."

"Where'd you learn that expression?"

"From your father."

"Oh. What makes you say we're not?"

Millicent thought a moment. "A couple of things. You don't act quite like yourself around her — you're more, I think the word is *maco*."

"Huh?"

"*Maco*. Tough, overly masculine . . ."

"Macho," Bart said, and laughed. "Hey, wait a minute . . ."

"And sometimes you lie to her."

"Like when?"

"Like the time you wanted to read instead of going out."

Bart stared at her. "How do you know about that?" he said.

"I heard you on the phone. Then I saw you take your copy of *Macbeth* and leave."

There was a long silence, and then Bart said, "Do you know what would happen if I told Lisa I wanted to hang out with *Macbeth* instead of her?"

"No. What would happen?"

"She'd think I was a grade-A nerd."

"A what?"

"A nerd. A person nobody would want to be caught dead with."

"That's ridiculous! What kind of person is she to think that?"

"It's not just her — it's everyone."

"Everyone? How could that be? When I was in school, the most popular boy in the class read three books a week and won the public speaking contest by reciting Hamlet's 'To be or not to be' speech."

"Well, things were different back then." He told her about Bart the Bookworm.

Another silence. Then Millicent said, "In 1914, I couldn't be a stuntwoman. Today I could. In 1914, you could've read *Macbeth* out loud to the whole school. Today you can't even tell your girlfriend about it. What a strange world!"

Bart didn't respond, and Millicent suddenly said, "You have to tell her, Bart. And all your friends. And your family too. It's no good worrying so much what people will think."

"Thank you, Dear Abby," Bart said dryly.

"But my name's Millie." The ghost sounded confused.

"Dear Abby's a writer who gives out advice."

"Oh, you were being sarcastic. I'm sorry if you think I'm being overbearing. It's just that I know what it's like not to let people see what you're really like."

"You know? How would you know?" Bart said sharply. "You told me you climbed trees and walked fences and got into trouble all you wanted to. It sounds like you were always yourself."

"I said I was good at those things — but I didn't say I did them."

Bart looked at her in surprise. "You didn't?"

"Not past age ten. You see, Mother and Father didn't approve. They wanted me to behave like a 'young lady,' so I tried to. But I wasn't very good at it — and even worse, I didn't enjoy it one bit. I felt as though I was lying all the time — to them, to my friends, and especially to myself. So, you see, Bart, I *do* know."

Bart didn't say a word, but he thought, Millie, you said you don't know why you came back as a ghost. But I have a feeling I do.

Chapter 15

It was pouring outside. The torrents of rain had turned the football field into one vast mud puddle. Worse, the wind was blasting so hard the goalposts were rattling. Bart looked out the window and frowned. Football games were hardly ever called on account of the weather, but it looked like this one might be.

When he got to the locker room, he undressed, taped up the ankle he'd injured in Rowan Woods, and began to suit up. It was a ritual he usually enjoyed. But today he wasn't concentrating on it. Instead he was thinking about Millie and what she'd told him the night before.

"Hey, you got steel knees these days?" Greg's voice interrupted his thoughts.

"Huh? What? No, why?" Bart answered in confusion.

"Because you forgot these," Greg said, tossing a pair of knee pads at him.

Bart caught them. "Man, I guess I'm out of it today. Must be the weather."

"Yeah. Hey, listen. I know you've been busy lately," Greg said, his tone implying some puzzlement at exactly what Bart had been busy with. "But do you think maybe you could grace us with your presence today at Yumby's?" He paused. "There's this new waitress there. Sixteen. Goes to DeForest, too. Red hair, green eyes. On Wednesday she dumped a banana split in my lap and pretended it was an accident. But I know better." He paused again. "I took her out last night, Bart. I think this one might be for real."

Bart smiled. "Hey, that's great," he said.

"So. How about it? Can you come to Yumby's today?"

Bart didn't say anything for a moment. Yes, he could go to Yumby's. Stryker was gone; he didn't have to rush home. But the truth was he didn't feel like going. He didn't feel like sitting in Yumby's with a crowd of people. He didn't feel like being Bart the Big Man. What he did feel like doing was going home and . . . and what? He felt funny admitting the truth to himself, because the truth was he wanted to go home and talk to Millie. "Uh, I, uh, I don't think I can today, Greg. I'm . . . uh . . . kind of beat. Sorry. How about next week sometime? Maybe we can . . . uh . . . double."

"Yeah. Okay," Greg said. His smile didn't quite conceal his disappointment. "You ready?"

"Yeah," Bart said.

Then the coach came in and told them that,

sure enough, the game was postponed until the next day.

Bart and Greg sighed and began to take off their uniforms.

Lisa met Bart at the door to the gym. He wished he didn't have to make an excuse about why he wasn't going to Yumby's to her, too. To his surprise, she told him first that she wanted to go home.

"Okay. I'll walk with you," he said.

They made their soggy way to Hexum Road.

When they reached Lisa's house, Bart said, "Well, I've got to . . ."

But Lisa cut him off. "I'm glad you didn't want to go to Yumby's today either. We haven't been alone together in a while. How does hot chocolate sound?"

"It sounds great, but . . . uh . . . Lisa, I can't come in right now. I'm really tired. I think I'm going to go home and, uh, take a nap."

"You are?"

"Yeah. It's this weather, I think."

Lisa looked even more disappointed than Greg had, so Bart quickly said, "Look, *Strange Dreams* is playing at the Royale tonight. We might as well go."

"Well, try not to sound so thrilled about it," Lisa retorted.

"I meant I thought we might go. Sorry, Lisa. I'm not all here today. I was all ready to clobber the Bombers, and then this rain . . ."

"Oh, I know how you feel," she responded

sympathetically. "But we will clobber them, Bart. We will. Tomorrow."

"Yeah. You're right. Pick you up at seven-thirty?"

She nodded.

He kissed her and sloshed on home.

When he got there, he found his mother muttering to herself and scraping what looked like batter off the kitchen floor. "Hi, Mom. What happened?" he asked, sidestepping the mess as he crossed to the refrigerator.

"Oh, hello, Bart. This was supposed to be a devil's food cake. I was just about to put it in the oven when it jumped out of my hands. Maybe a little devil was inside it. There." She dumped a wad of gooey paper towels into the garbage pail. "Was your game postponed?"

"Yeah," answered Bart, peeling an orange he'd taken from the fridge. "It's going to be tomorrow if the weather's okay."

"Well, at least now your father and I will be able to see it. He couldn't take off for another Friday afternoon game, you know."

"Mom!" Leanne cried, bursting into the room. "Have you seen my black hat? The flat one with the round brim? I've got a rehearsal and I want to wear it."

"No, I haven't. But I'm not surprised you can't find it considering the state your room is in."

"I didn't leave it in my room. I left it right on the bannister."

"Leanne," Mrs. Hawkins sighed. "How many

times have I told you that the bannister is not a hat rack?"

Leanne frowned and turned to Bart. "How about you? Did you take it?"

"What would I want with your dumb old hat?" Bart retorted, but without as much pep as he usually put into it.

"Where's Dusty? Maybe he took it."

"He's at Manny's and I'm sure no one took your hat, Leanne," Mrs. Hawkins said. She sounded irritated.

"Well, it didn't just disappear," Leanne snapped, and stomped out of the room.

There was a moment of silence in the kitchen, pierced suddenly by a startled *"Oh"* that came from the hall.

"Leanne? Is something wrong?" Mrs. Hawkins called.

Leanne reappeared in the kitchen doorway, a flat black hat with a round brim sitting squarely on her head. Her face was slightly pale.

"Good, you found it," Mrs. Hawkins said. "I'll bet it was right in front of your eyes, too."

"I was looking at the table near the stairs and it . . . it . . . jumped out at me," Leanne said.

Bart snorted and ate a section of his orange.

"Yes, that's what I just said," said Mrs. Hawkins.

"No, I mean it really jumped out at me — from *under* the table. It was like an unseen hand moved it."

Bart looked up sharply.

"Well, perhaps the same devil that got into

my cake batter got into your hat," Mrs. Hawkins said in an amused voice.

Bart was not amused. There was a cold spot between his shoulder blades, as though someone were touching him with a single icy finger. He shuddered.

Suddenly, Leanne yelled, "Ahhh!" and pointed at the floor.

Bart jumped out of his chair.

Mrs. Hawkins was startled too — especially when the small brown mouse Leanne was pointing at ran right over her foot.

Mrs. Hawkins and Bart started to laugh. "There's your 'unseen hand,' Leanne," she said.

"Mighty Mouse!" said Bart with a chortle. The cold spot had disappeared from his back.

"I don't think it's funny. I *hate* mice," Leanne complained.

"Well then, you won't mind stopping at Plover's Hardware on your way to Rocky's and picking up some Rodent-Ridder for me, will you?" Mrs. Hawkins said.

"But Mom, I've got a rehearsal. . . ."

"Yes, and I've got a P.T.A. meeting," Mrs. Hawkins said, looking at the clock. "I'll see you both later." She dashed out of the room.

"How come you're so afraid of mice, Donuthead? You perform with a bunch of them," Bart said.

"Oh shut up, Barfface," Leanne snapped and she left too.

Bart polished off his orange, stood up, and stretched. He was alone in the house now — and at last he could do what he wanted to. He marched out of the kitchen and upstairs to his room.

"Millie! Hey, Millicent! Come on out and play!" he called lightly. He waited expectantly, but no shimmering form appeared, no silvery glow.

"Millie? Can you hear me? Are you asleep?" he teased, then wondered if ghosts did in fact sleep. "Millie?"

Five minutes passed. Ten, and there was still no sign of the ghost. Bart felt let down. He glanced out the window. The rain had let up a bit, but the sky was still leaden and a brisk wind was coming up, whistling under the eaves. He sighed. What a dreary day this was turning out to be. Maybe I should go over to Lisa's after all, he thought. Or to Greg's. Or I could read — nobody's here to bother me. But somehow none of those things, not even reading, was appealing. He let out a big yawn. Jeez, I *am* tired after all, he thought. He sat down on the bed. Maybe I *will* take a nap. He stretched out. His eyelids felt very heavy. He closed them.

The sun was shining brightly. But he hardly noticed it. He was concentrating instead on the football in his hand and the beefy tackle charging at him. He faked a handoff to the fullback and ran, ran, ran with the ball himself. Touchdown! "We won! We won!" someone yelled.

The next thing Bart knew he was being hoisted up on the shoulders of two large guards and carried off the field to the sounds of cheers.

He turned to wave at the crowd, and there, some twenty yards away, he saw a familiar figure. She was tall and slim and dressed in an old-fashioned white frock. She was gliding toward him in slow motion, saying something he couldn't make out.

"What? I can't understand you," he said. "What are you saying?"

Her mouth kept moving, but he still couldn't hear her.

Then he was in the locker room, where a flock of reporters had gathered.

"So, Hawk, how does it feel to win the Super Bowl?" one of them asked.

"Yeah, tell us, Hawk."

"It feels great!" he said. He reached up to pull his helmet off and he groaned. Suddenly, he knew what was coming next. He took his hand away and turned his face from the reporters. There, at the edge of the crowd, taller than everyone else, as though she were standing on a box — or hovering in the air — was the same figure in the white dress. Her lips formed words, but Bart was still deaf to them. He started to walk toward her. And she disappeared.

He turned back to the reporters. "It feels great!" he said again and took off his helmet. He ran a hand across his scalp.

"He's got no hair! The Hawk's got no hair!"

"Then we'll have to call him the Eagle. The *Bald* Eagle!"

The laughter began, swelling and swelling until Bart clapped his hands over his ears.

"Bart the Bald! Bart the Bald! Bart the . . ."

"No! No! Leave me alone! Leave me alone!" he yelled.

"Bart! Bart! Wake up! Come on, please. Wake up!"

"No, leave me . . . uh . . . what?" He blinked. He was in his bedroom. Someone was hovering over him. A girl. *The* girl, in the white dress. But so pale and wispy he could barely see her. What's she doing here, he wondered. What . . .

"Bart, you've got to help. He's back and — oh!"

"Millie?" He blinked again. There was no one there. He sat up. His head felt logy, and everything was indistinct in the gray light. "Millie? Was that you?" He wasn't sure whether he'd really seen her in the room or if that had been part of his bad dream too.

Suddenly there was a rap on his door.

"Who is it?" he asked.

"Dusty."

"Millie?" he whispered. But after there was no response, he switched on his bedside light and called, "Yeah. Okay. Come in."

The door opened and his brother entered. "Mom said to tell you it's time for dinner," Dusty said.

"Hmmm. Oh, okay," Bart replied.

"You better come right down. Mom's in a bad mood. I think she got into an argument at the P.T.A. meeting. Then she lost her umbrella.

And now she's mad at me. It was my turn to set the table. I put down Leanne's water glass and it bounced off the table just like it was a frog or something. Really weird. But Mom didn't believe me. She thinks I did it. So come right down or she'll be angry at you too."

"Right," Bart said, and followed his brother downstairs.

"For once I'd like us to eat on time," Mrs. Hawkins said tightly as the boys sat down at the dining room table. She stalked off into the kitchen.

Bart caught Leanne's eye and made a face like a gnawing mouse at her. She made a rude gesture in return.

"Leanne, watch those finger twitches," Mr. Hawkins said.

Mrs. Hawkins returned, carrying a roasted chicken on a platter. She set it next to the wooden salad bowl on the table and sat down. "Now, let's say grace." She bowed her head and began reciting the prayer aloud.

Everyone else lowered their heads too, but Bart only kept his down for a moment. He'd heard a faint rattling. He looked up at the table and his mouth fell open. The chicken was standing on one end weaving slowly back and forth.

Oh no. No! He's back. That's what Millie was trying to tell me. Stryker's back — if he ever left at all.

". . . which we are about to receive from thy bounty . . ." Mrs. Hawkins was finishing the prayer. Any moment now they'd look up and see the chicken, which was already half off the platter and advancing toward Mr. Hawkins.

Bart jumped to his feet. "Avaunt, ye ancestral manes!" he yelled and grabbed the chicken.

Everyone looked up at him, puzzled or annoyed.

"Bart, what kind of joke is this?" Mrs. Hawkins asked.

"Are you all right, son?" asked Mr. Hawkins.

Leanne giggled.

Bart stood there clutching the greasy, slippery fowl. "Uh . . . no . . . I must've . . . uh . . . dozed off for a minute. I was dreaming about . . . about the Super Bowl, and I . . ." His voice trailed off.

"You thought the chicken was a football?" asked Dusty.

Thanks, little brother, Bart thought. "Uh . . . yeah, I . . . I guess I did," he said with what he hoped was an appropriately sheepish tone.

"He's trying to find a new way to *pass* the chicken," Leanne said.

Dusty and Mr. Hawkins laughed, and Bart forced himself to join in.

Mrs. Hawkins didn't. "Oh Lord, what next?" she said.

Bart, gingerly setting the chicken back in place, was thinking the very same question — and dreading the answer to it.

Chapter 16

The game against the Blitzberg Bombers was a disaster, and Bart knew why; he hadn't been able to keep his mind on the game. He kept worrying about Stryker. The "ancestral manes" business hadn't done the trick at all — at least not on the poltergeist. Since the night before, the noisy ghost had gotten worse. At breakfast he sent Bart's bowl of cereal crashing to the floor, and he would've tipped over a pitcher of orange juice if Bart hadn't caught it in time. He also literally pulled the rug out from under Bart's feet and sent an umbrella whizzing past his brother's head. Luckily, Bart was behind Dusty, and he had to pretend he'd done it as a joke. But even more upsetting was the fact that although the invocation hadn't worked on Stryker, it seemed to have chased away Millie and her friends. Bart hadn't seen her at all since her brief appearance the day before, even though he'd been up most of the night waiting for her. So, all in all, Bart was one unhappy guy.

His teammates were kind to him after the terrible football game. "Those Bombers are tough," everyone said.

Coach Dibbetts was not so sympathetic. "What was going on in here, Hawkins?" he asked, tapping Bart's noggin. "You closed for repairs or something? You called play forty-six when you should've called thirty-eight, and you fumbled the snap twice."

"I'm sorry," Bart said. "I wasn't concentrating." There was no use trying to pass the buck or lie his way out of it with Coach Dibbetts. You couldn't fool the man no matter how hard you tried.

"Yeah, well, that's for sure. It's also for sure what you weren't doing Marty Peterson was," the coach said. "And you can bet your cleats the Surgeons' quarterback will be, too, so you better have a grand reopening real soon or the Phantoms can kiss the championship good-bye." He tapped Bart's head again.

Bart didn't say anything. He just nodded.

Coach Dibbetts' seamed face uncreased a bit. "Is something bothering you, Hawk? You got problems at home?"

Yeah, he wanted to say. I've got a poltergeist I've got to get rid of so that nine other ghosts can stay in my house. He could imagine the look on the coach's face if he said that. He wiped his hand across his mouth to cover a smile. "No. No problems," he said.

"Good. Then get that brain back into shape

so we can slaughter the Surgeons next week."
Coach Dibbetts smacked Bart on the rump.

"Right, Coach," Bart said, and ran off to take a shower.

His family wasn't as rough on him as the coach, though his father's disappointment was more than apparent. "What happened today, son?" Mr. Hawkins asked. "You didn't play like you usually do."

"I don't know," Bart lied.

"I thought you played well, Bart," Mrs. Hawkins said. "That was a very long throw you made in the third quarter."

"It got intercepted, Mom," Dusty explained.

"I know, but he still threw it so far."

Bart had to smile. With all the football games his mother had seen, she still didn't quite understand the game. He also knew she was trying to make up for her bad mood the day before.

Lisa came up and joined them. She was still in her cheerleading uniform. She put her arm around Bart's waist. "Hi, Mr. and Mrs. Hawkins. Hello, Dusty." Then, giving Bart a hug, she said, "Tough luck today, Bart. Those Bombers are brutal! But don't worry, we'll slice up the Surgeons next week. You still can break Flip Walonski's record."

"Yeah," Bart said, but he found himself wishing she'd just be quiet for a change instead of giving him a pep talk.

"Come on," she said. "You'll feel better after one of Yumby's hot fudge sundaes. Today I'll treat."

"Howard, Dusty, we'd better get on home and start working on those new bookshelves," Mrs. Hawkins said. "Have fun, kids. We'll see you later."

"Right, Mom," Bart began. He watched them turn away, then he remembered. He couldn't let them go home alone with Stryker on the loose. "Uh . . . wait a minute. I think I'll . . . I mean, I'm coming with you."

"You are?" said Mr. Hawkins and Lisa at the same time.

"Yeah. I've got to . . . I mean, I'm not . . ."

"Bart, you aren't getting sick, are you?" his mother asked. "You didn't act quite yourself last night, falling asleep at the dinner table the way you did."

"Uh . . . I don't know. My . . . uh . . . nose is a little stuffy, and my . . . er . . . head kind of . . . aches." He drooped his head and shoulders a bit.

"Oh dear, it sounds like you're getting the flu." His mother put her hand to his forehead.

"Oh, Bart. How awful. I should've known there was something wrong when you said you were sleepy yesterday afternoon. You better get home and get right into bed," Lisa said, outmothering his mother.

"Yeah, I think I better go home." He gave a little cough.

"I'll call you later, to see how you're feeling," Lisa said.

Drooping further, Bart trailed after his parents. Well, Hawkins, he thought, if you don't make it in football, there's another career for you that you're getting pretty good at. Acting.

When they got back to their house, Bart got to test his acting ability further. He couldn't go straight to bed, as Lisa had insisted. He had to keep his eyes open for Stryker. So he convinced his parents he was feeling better ("Maybe I had an allergic reaction or something," he said) and wanted to help with the bookshelves. It was a good thing he did, too, because otherwise he wouldn't have been there to grab the hammer as it sailed toward the wall. He also rescued two boxes of nails and a can of varnish. The one thing he couldn't do anything about was the intense cold in the room.

"Howard, I think we'd better turn up the heat. It's like an icebox in here," his mother said.

"I already turned it up to seventy degrees," Mr. Hawkins said.

"Well, perhaps the radiator's not working right." Mrs. Hawkins crossed over to it. "Hmm, it's hot enough." She shivered. "Maybe I'm still chilled from the game. It was rather brisk out there." She turned around in Bart's direction and noticed he had the varnish in his hand and that his hand was raised above his head.

"Bart, what are you doing?" she asked.

"I'm . . . uh . . . weight training. Coach Dibbetts says you should develop your muscles all the time using everyday objects."

"Sounds like good advice," Mr. Hawkins said.

With a grunt he lifted a heavy plank of wood onto the brackets he'd installed. "There. Finished. Let's clean this up. Then I think *I'm* going to bed."

They cleaned up, and Mr. Hawkins, stretching, said, "Okay. Nap time."

"Not for me. I'm full of energy. I think I'll go to work on Mrs. Posnick's dress before dinnertime. Want to help me, Dusty?" Mrs. Hawkins teased.

"No thanks, Mom. I'm going to work on my entry for the *Mathematical Games and Puzzles* 'Best Puzzle of the Year' contest."

"What about you, Bart?" asked Mrs. Hawkins. "You feeling funny again? You look a little pale."

Bart was indeed pale. His family was about to split up into separate rooms, and he had no idea where Stryker might show up next. "Uh, no. I'm fine. I . . . you know, it was really fun working on these shelves together. I . . . we don't do enough as a family. Why don't we . . . uh . . . do something else together? How about a Monopoly game?"

"Huh?" said Dusty, looking at him as if he were crazy.

"Gee, Bart, I don't know. I'm really kind of bushed," Mr. Hawkins began.

"Why, Bart," Mrs. Hawkins said. "What a nice idea!" She smiled tenderly at her son.

Bart smiled back and wished his insides were smiling too.

* * *

They played Monopoly until dinnertime. Leanne came in midway through the game and Bart (with Mrs. Hawkins' help) insisted they start all over again. Bart was the banker, which was a good thing, because several times the money shuffled together by itself (or rather by Stryker) — the tens, ones, thousands getting all mixed up. But Bart was quick enough to get the bills back in place without anyone noticing.

The game lasted so long that Mr. Hawkins suggested they all go out to eat rather than cook at home, which suited Bart just fine.

They piled into the car, Bart trying to ignore both the hostile or puzzled stares from Leanne and Dusty and the happy beams from his mother. The restaurant Mr. Hawkins took them to was one of Bart's favorites, but he only picked at his food. He was worried about what would happen when they returned to the house.

He was worrying so much he didn't hear Gillian Landers say hello to him until she said it twice. Finally he looked up. "Oh, hi," he said.

"Bart, introduce us to your friend," Mrs. Hawkins said.

"Oh, sure. Gillian, these are my parents, my brother, Dusty, my sister, Leanne." He lowered his head back to his plate.

Gillian remained standing there.

"Would you like to join us for dessert, dear?" Mrs. Hawkins asked.

Bart looked up again and tried to signal no to his mother. She didn't notice.

"Oh, I don't know," said Gillian. "I'm with

my parents. They're just leaving. How would I get home?"

"We'll drive you."

"Oh. Okay. I'll go tell them," Gillian said swiftly, and left.

"Mom, didn't you see me shaking my head?" Bart asked.

"She didn't hear it rattle," said Leanne.

"Ha ha. Very funny, Donutbrain."

Gillian hurried back. Mr. Hawkins pulled out a chair for her right between himself and Bart.

"Too bad about the game today, Bart," Gillian said, leaning toward him.

"Uh, yeah," Bart answered. He was back to worrying about the rest of the evening.

"You did your best. But the rest of the team didn't."

"Uh, sure."

"They don't always pull their weight, do they?"

"Uh, right."

"And . . ."

"Hello, Bart. I see you're feeling better," a voice cut in.

Bart looked up. Lisa was standing right next to him. Her mouth was smiling, but her eyes weren't.

"And Gillian. How nice. Are you having a good time?"

"Oh yes," Gillian answered.

"How wonderful for you," said Lisa.

"Are you here with your parents?" Mr. Hawkins asked her.

"Yes," she replied politely. "We're sitting right over there."

Mr. Hawkins turned and waved. Lisa's parents waved back.

"They thought they'd treat me to dinner since I don't have a date tonight," Lisa said sweetly.

"Uh, Lise." Bart stood up. "Can I talk with you for a minute?"

"Certainly. Tomorrow morning at eleven sharp. Good night, everyone. Enjoy your dessert. You too, Gillian." She sauntered away.

"Sweet girl," said Mr. Hawkins.

"I don't think she likes me very much," Gillian whispered to Bart.

"Boy, are you in hot water," Dusty said to him.

Leanne just laughed.

"Excuse me," Bart said, getting up and heading for the men's room. Millie, wherever you are, he said to himself in the mirror. What am I supposed to do now?

Chapter 17

Bart didn't get any advice from Millicent. In fact, she didn't appear on Saturday at all. But praying she wasn't gone for good, he kept up his attempts to prevent his family from realizing there was a poltergeist in the house.

When they returned from dinner (minus Leanne, who had another gig to go to), Bart came up with the idea of watching old home movies. His parents loved the idea. Dusty didn't. He spent the time trying to work on his puzzle by the light of the projector bulb. But at least he stayed with them. Everything went okay during the films, and Bart was beginning to relax. But then his mother decided to go make popcorn. Bart jumped up. He didn't know whether to follow her or to stay in the rec room. He stayed. "I'll rewind the film, Dad," he offered, as his father sorted through film cans to find "Bart's First Year."

"Okay," Mr. Hawkins said.

Bart slipped the reels into rewind position,

flicked a switch, and suddenly found himself wrapped in fifty feet of Super 8 film. He yelped. Dusty and his father looked up.

"Good grief. What did you do?" Mr. Hawkins asked.

"Nothing. I mean, I don't know," Bart played dumb. He knew Stryker was at it again.

"Well, don't move. You'll rip it." Slowly, Mr. Hawkins unwound the celluloid from his son's neck.

There were no further mishaps, and everyone soon went to their bedrooms. That's when Bart really got tense. What if Stryker threw his parents' clock across the room? Or if he made Dusty's old *Star Wars* figures get down from their shelf and start acting out their own movie? And then there was Leanne. When she came home, would her hat hop off her head and fly like a Frisbee all around the hall? So, instead of going to bed, Bart paced the house, pausing at doors, feeling for icy drafts and praying that Stryker would stay away — and that Millie would return.

Leanne came home and found him standing in the kitchen, inspecting the broom closet. "Thinking of cleaning the house?" she asked.

"Uh . . . no. I thought I heard that mouse in here."

"Ew." Leanne gave a little shudder.

Bart crossed to the refrigerator, opened it, and took out the milk. He knew Leanne wouldn't ask him any further questions if she thought he was just there for a midnight snack. "How was your gig?" he asked, pouring himself a glass.

"Pretty good."

"I wonder if your secret admirer was there."

Leanne squinted at him. "What secret admirer?"

"The one who loved you at Folger."

"If he's from Folger, what would he be doing at Hobby Academy here in Sprocketsville?"

"I never said he was from Folger."

Leanne was quiet a minute. "This ... uh ... person. He's not one of your idiot jock friends, is he?"

"No, I wouldn't say he was one of my jock friends."

Leanne nibbled her lip. Bart knew she was dying to ask him who it was, but instead she said, "Hey, pour me a glass of that too, will you?"

Bart obeyed and handed it to her.

She took a sip and giggled.

"What's so funny?"

"I was just remembering something that happened at the gig tonight."

"Yeah?" Bart said. But he was feeling distracted. *I ought to check upstairs again. Make sure he's not doing something in the hall. . . .*

"After we finished, this pudgy, baby-faced kid came up to me. He was all red in the face and he couldn't look me in the eye. But then he took a big breath and said, real fast, 'I just want to tell you that you are a superlative singer. Your power, range, and vibrancy far surpass that of Linda Ronstadt.' Then he gave me this.". She pulled a small book out of her jacket pocket and gave it to Bart. The title read *Haunted Houses and How to Find Them*. "He said it wasn't very — what was that word — *erudite*, that's it, but that it was highly entertaining. Then he ran away. Funny, huh?"

Bart spit his milk back into his glass so he wouldn't choke on it. "Funny," he said.

"Maybe he was teasing me the way the other kids have about our house."

"I don't think so," Bart said.

"Why?" Leanne asked, suddenly suspicious. "You know this guy or something?"

"Me? Would I hang out with a nerd like that?"

"I guess not," Leanne said. "But then why else would he give me this?"

"Uh, I don't know," Bart said. "Maybe he thinks you're interested in parapsychology."

"Para-what?"

"Parapsychology. The study of psychic phenomena."

Leanne shrugged. Then she laughed again. "He was really funny. He had this squeaky voice, but he talked like a college professor. He was a nerd all right. But . . . sweet."

Well, Arvie, Bart thought, maybe you don't have that many yards to go for a touchdown after all.

Bang! Both Bart and Leanne jumped and whirled around. Then they relaxed. Bart had left the broom closet open and a mop had fallen out of it on to the floor. He picked it up, propped it back in the closet, and closed the door.

"I'm going to bed," Leanne said, rinsing out her glass.

"Good," said Bart. "I mean, good night."

She went up to her room, and Bart continued his rounds of the house.

The next day, despite his growing fatigue, he organized more family activities, cleaning out the basement, straightening up the yard, and even, out of sheer desperation, helping his mother bake bread when his father went over to a neighbor's house to look at his stopped-up sink. Dusty escaped to his friend Manny's house, which was fine with Bart. Leanne, on the other hand, stayed in her room, writing an overdue book report for English and making Bart extremely nervous lest Stryker pay her a visit there. Several of Bart's friends called during the morning, but he hurriedly told them he was working out and couldn't talk. However, at eleven o'clock on the dot, he did risk leaving his parents alone in the basement to phone Lisa.

"Explain," she said curtly.

"Uh . . . ah . . . my dad decided to take us out to eat. I was feeling better by then, so I came along."

"Gillian."

"She was at the same restaurant with her parents. She came over to say hi and Mom invited her to join us. That's all."

"It is? If you were feeling better, how come you didn't call and tell me so? I tried calling you just before we left for dinner, but you and your family must've already gone."

"I . . . um . . . I'm sorry. I meant to call, but . . ."

"But what? You've been giving me a lot of 'buts' lately. What's going on?"

"Nothing's going on."

"Okay. Then come over, Right now."

"Uh . . . I can't right now. I'd like to, but . . . I mean, I can't."

"Why not?"

"I'm helping my folks clean out the basement."

"Okay, then after you finish."

"Uh, then we're working on the yard."

"When will you be done with that?"

"I don't know."

"Okay, then I'll come over to your place and help too."

"No, you don't want to do that."

"Why not?" Lisa was getting more and more irritated.

"Because it's . . . uh . . . you know, it isn't fun. It's dirty work."

"I can think of a lot dirtier work — and you can too," Lisa snapped, and hung up.

Bart looked at the dead receiver and sighed.

Then he ran back to the basement just in time to catch a stack of old *National Geographic*s that was sailing through the air.

"I guess it *is* time to chuck those out," his

mother said, turning around just after he'd caught the magazines.

"Yeah," he said, dumping them into a garbage bag and collapsing beside them.

Later in the day his mother went to visit a friend, and Leanne, having finally finished her report, went to rehearse, leaving Bart and his father alone in the house to watch the football game. Bart wished his dad would leave too, but there was no way to get him to give up his Sunday ritual. So Bart sat with him, scarcely watching the game. Then the doorbell rang. He heard it, but didn't know whether to get up and answer it or to stay and let his father do it.

It rang again.

"Clipping! He wasn't clipping," his father yelled at the TV. "That referee is blind. . . . Hey, was that the bell?"

"Uh . . . yeah," Bart said.

"Are you going to answer it, or are you waiting for somebody else to do it?" Mr. Hawkins asked in an amused voice.

"Uh . . . I'll get it." He ran up the stairs and into the hall as fast as he could and flung open the door, hoping to get rid of whoever was there quickly.

On the porch were Greg and Tom.

"You feeling better?" Greg asked. "Lisa said you had the flu."

"Yeah, I'm better."

"Good. We were passing by and thought we'd drop in to watch the game," Greg said. "Okay with you?"

"Uh . . . well . . . uh . . ." Bart wanted to scream, No! Go home. This house is haunted! But not a single good excuse popped into his head. Greg was his best friend. He knew Bart and his father almost always watched the game on Sundays, and he'd watched it with them countless times himself.

"Uh . . . yeah. Sure. Come in," Bart said, opening the door wider.

Greg and Tom followed him down to the rec room.

"Jeez, you are blind!" Mr. Hawkins was yelling. "That guy was offsides!" He looked up. "Hi, Greg. Hello, Tom. Take a pew."

Greg and Tom sat down. Bart did too, in a chair behind them so he could survey the room without being noticed.

The second quarter ended, and Mr. Hawkins went to the john.

"You hear about Tony? He got grounded," Greg said, turning around to Bart.

"Uh . . . yeah?" Bart said, scanning the wall behind Greg. "Was he drunk again?"

"No. He borrowed his dad's car."

"Borrowed his dad's car? Jeez, he must be crazy. He doesn't have a license. Why'd he do it?" Bart looked directly at Greg. His friend had gotten his attention.

"It was a bet he made with Bob. His dad wouldn't have found out, though, if Tony hadn't scraped the car against a hydrant and taken off a lot of paint."

"Oh man, what a turkey!"

"Hey, Bart. Do those pictures always do that?" Tom cut in.

"What do you . . ." Bart followed Tom's gaze and gasped.

Two small paintings of airplanes he'd done in sixth grade were spinning around and around in circles on the wall behind his head.

"Cut it out!" he yelled.

The pictures immediately stopped spinning. Bart breathed a sigh of relief. Then he realized that Greg and Tom were staring at him. He forced out a feeble laugh. "Ha ha. My . . . uh . . . brother. Dusty. Always trying out some weird invention."

"That was a pretty good one. How'd he do it without being here to run it?" Tom asked.

"I don't know," Bart answered.

"I didn't think Dusty was into science," Greg said. "I thought he was a math maniac."

"Yeah. Well, math, science, you know, all that stuff," Bart said swiftly. "Hey, listen, guys. Why don't we go outside and throw a few. I need to work on my arm. I really stank against the Bombers."

"But the game," Tom nodded at the TV.

"We've got to work on *our* game," Bart replied, trying to sound like the leader he was supposed to be.

"Okay, Hawk. I'm game," said Greg with a smile. "Besides, it's freezing in here."

"Yeah. Boiler trouble." Bart led his friends upstairs.

"You guys leaving?" Mr. Hawkins said, meeting them at he door.

Dad! I forgot about him, Bart thought. I'm losing my mind. He can't . . . But we can't . . . Oh, Millie, Millie, how'd I let you get me into this?

"Bart says we need to practice," Tom said.

"Yeah, Dad. Say, why don't you come too?" Bart said.

"And miss the game?"

"It's a lousy game, and it's half over anyway. Come on, Dad, please."

"Yeah, you're right. It *is* a lousy game — and I could use some exercise myself. Okay. Let's go."

Safe, Bart thought with relief. But the relief was short-lived, because he knew if he didn't figure out some way soon to drive the poltergeist out of his house, he would be the one to be driven out — right out of his mind.

Chapter 18

By late Sunday afternoon, Bart, pale and hollow-eyed, was beginning to resemble a ghost himself. He hadn't slept for two nights, he was still worried about Millie, and in one weekend he'd done more physical labor than he usually did in a week.

He sat on the edge of his bed with his head in his hands. By a stroke of luck, his mother's car had died while she was trying to leave her friend's house. His father had taken his car to meet her and see if he could get the Silver Syphon, as Mrs. Hawkins called it, to go. Leanne and Dusty were still gone, so Bart was alone. He didn't know for how long he would be, but he hoped it was enough time for a catnap, because if he didn't get forty winks soon, he would fall asleep at the dinner table for real.

He sank onto his back, drawing his legs up on the mattress. Oh, Lord, I can't keep this up. Maybe I should try another library. There's a bigger one in Blitzberg. Maybe there're some books there I haven't checked out that'll tell me how to get rid of this pest. "Oh, Lord," he groaned aloud. "Maybe . . ." He couldn't form another thought. The room turned a pleasant gray-green, the way it always did when he was about to fall asleep. His eyelids drooped.

"Bart?"

His lids shot open.

There, floating before him, was Millicent.

Bart felt a surge of joy. "You're back!" he shouted. "What happened? Where were you?"

"In the attic. When you blurted out that 'ancestral manes' business, Old Man Koral, who was in the pantry at the time, got a terrible jolt."

"Oh no," Bart moaned.

"The rest of us weren't in earshot, and none of us suffered even the mildest discomfort. So we decided to make sure we couldn't hear you. We stayed in the attic until an hour ago, when Old Man Koral realized the jolt he'd received hadn't come from the invocation at all, but from the garlic bulbs he'd been standing next to in the pantry."

"Garlic? Garlic bothers ghosts? I thought it worked on vampires," Bart said.

"It does. But when he was alive, Old Man Koral used to be allergic to garlic, and apparently he still is. There are some things even being dead won't cure," Millicent answered with a laugh.

"What was Old Man Koral doing in the pantry anyway?"

"Trying to scare away the mouse that was plaguing your mother and sister."

"That was nice of him."

"Oh, he *is* nice." She lowered her voice. "A bit dotty, but nice."

Bart laughed. Then, shyly, he said, "I was worried I wouldn't see you again."

"I missed you too, Bart," Millicent said.

There was a pause; then he said, "I had a funny dream. Well, not *funny* funny. Weird. I've had it before. But this time *you* were in it."

"What was it about?"

Bart told her the last Bart the Bald dream. Then he said, "What do you think it's about?"

Millicent paused a minute, then said, "You haven't told Lisa or anyone else about Bart the Bookworm, have you?"

"No. But what does that have to do with my dream?"

"I think that when you tell them what you're really like — when you stop worrying so much about how you look to other people — you'll stop having the dream."

Bart was disappointed with Millicent's reply. But instead of telling her that, he said, "I don't think I'm going to be telling Lisa anything much for a while. She's mad at me."

"Why?"

"Because I've been too busy trying to keep my family from finding out about Stryker to spend any time with her." Bart knew that that wasn't the entire reason he wasn't spending time with Lisa, but he went on. "I can't keep it up, Millie.

That lousy poltergeist's gotten worse. It's only been sheer luck that I've managed to cover his tracks. But I can't be everywhere. Today when my friends were here was nearly the end. I can't keep it up."

"Hmmm," said Millicent. "Every time Stryker has done something lately — have you been there?"

"Yes. That's why I said it's been sheer luck..."

"No, not sheer luck. More likely Stryker's perverse sense of humor."

"What do you mean?"

"He's enjoying watching you dashing around, trying to cover up his tracks."

"You mean he only acts up when I'm around so he can get a kick out of running me ragged?"

"Yes. I think that's a good way of putting it."

"That son of a . . ." Bart leaped to his feet. "I'm going to get rid of that sucker no matter what it takes. He wants to play games, does he? He hasn't seen the games I . . ."

In that instant, the room went cold, Bart's closet door flew open, and a football zoomed out at him. He caught it. "Very funny, Stryker. Very funny. You like to play football, huh? What position? Running back? Guard? Or tack — oof!"

Bart was knocked hard to the floor. The ball was whisked out of his hands. It took him a minute to catch his breath. He stood up, and immediately, the ball was thrown back to him. He took a few steps back and tried to drop the ball, but he was tackled again even harder before he could get it out of his hands.

"Stryker! That's enough!" Millicent ordered.

Bart sat up, woozy. Once again, the poltergeist threw the ball at him. He tried not to catch it, but it ended up in his hands anyway. He refused to stand up, but an unseen hand pinched his butt and pulled his hair and shirt collar so that he was on his feet again before he realized it.

"Stryker, stop it!" Millicent commanded again.

Bart stumbled toward the door and managed to open it just before he got tackled for a third time.

His nose banged the floor. "Ouch," he said, touching it. It was bleeding. He needed a handkerchief.

The poltergeist let him get one from his dresser drawer before tossing him the ball again. Bart was beginning to feel scared. Stryker was playing rough now, really rough.

Suddenly, Millicent called, "Okay. I want to play too." She was hovering out in the hall signaling to him.

In a flash, Bart realized what she was up to. He threw a short pass at her before Stryker could tackle him and ran toward the door.

Millicent stepped forward, reaching transparent arms toward the ball. But she didn't catch it. The pass was intercepted right at the doorjamb. And at the exact same moment, Bart grabbed the knob and slammed the door as hard as he could.

There was an unearthly cry that rose and rose in pitch until Bart had to clap his hands over his ears. "Stop! Stop!" he screamed.

And then it did. Bart took his hands away. The room was warm again and it smelled faintly of something like old fish.

"Millie? Are you okay? Millie?" Bart flung open the door. The football was lying there. He picked it up. "Millie?"

"I'm here," said a voice behind him.

He whirled around. She was rippling next to his bed. "How'd you get back in the room?"

"I'm a ghost, remember? I walked through the wall."

"Oh."

"Millie, we did it. We caught that sucker between door and doorpost just like that book said to do. And he's gone. Really gone. This time I'm sure of it."

"Oh, Bart. I hope so. I really hope so."

"Did you hear that scream? And smell that odor. Pee-*yu*."

"I can't smell anything."

"Well, take my word for it. It's the smell of putrefied poltergeist."

Downstairs, the front door opened. "Leanne! Bart! Anybody home?"

"It's your parents. I must go," Millicent said, and vanished.

"Come back later so we can celebrate," Bart

whispered and went out into the hall. "I'm here, Mom," he called from the top of the stairs.

"Good. You can help me with dinner. I had an exhausting day."

"Okay," Bart said, and he was surprised to realize that his own exhaustion was gone. He was feeling invigorated — as invigorated as if he'd just won a football game.

The rest of the day went well. There were no problems at dinner. Afterward, Bart called up Greg and invited himself over to his house.

"You seemed kind of jumpy today," Greg said.

"Yeah, well . . ." Bart answered.

"That was weird — those pictures spinning around. Your brother's getting into strange stuff."

"I'll let you in on a little secret," Bart said. "That wasn't Dusty's doing after all. It was our friendy neighborhood poltergeist."

Greg laughed.

Bart laughed too. He hadn't felt so good in weeks.

He whistled all the way back to his house. There he found both his parents fast asleep in front of the TV.

He padded softly into the kitchen. Dusty, in his pajamas, was finishing a piece of chocolate cake.

"Hey, little brother. How's the prize-winning puzzle coming along?"

Dusty gave his brother a fish-eyed stare. Then he said, "Pretty good. I finished it today."

"Great. It's been a good day for finishing things. . . . Leanne home yet?"

"Yeah. She went to bed already."

"Hmmm, sounds like a good idea. You coming too? You don't want Mom and Dad to catch you up."

"They're too out of it to catch me. Mom said she was glad you were so enthusiastic about working around the house, but she hopes you won't get so enthusiastic too often."

Bart chuckled. "Oh, I doubt I will."

Dusty gave him a puzzled look, then shrugged.

"Well, good night," Bart said.

"Good night," Dusty responded.

Whistling, Bart made his way upstairs. He washed his face, brushed his teeth, and went into his room. He turned on the light, got out his pajamas, and put them on. At last, he thought, I'm going to get a good night's sleep. He pulled down the cover, turned to look in the mirror, and had to clutch hold of his night table for support.

Scrawled across the glass in big black letters were the words "Who's the sucker now?"

Chapter 19

Bart cut school the next day. He called in sick, faking his father's voice. He'd never done that before, and he didn't enjoy doing it now. He especially hated missing football practice. He felt he was letting the team down — particularly with the big game against the Shamashugee Surgeons just four days away. If they lost that game, they'd be tied with the Surgeons for the championship, and they'd have to have a play-off. But the situation in his house was even more desperate. Catching Stryker "betwixt door and doorpost" had not only not worked, but Bart had an uneasy feeling the poltergeist had grown even more powerful than before. And probably more annoyed as well. He'd be out to fix Bart but good this time — if Bart didn't fix him first.

So that was why, after another sleepless night, Bart was sitting in the bus to Blitzberg instead of in Ms. Beardsley's English class. The Blitzberg library was twice the size of

Sprocketsville's, and Bart hoped to find some books on ghosts he hadn't read before.

He did, in fact, find two, and he read them eagerly, praying he'd find a solution to the poltergeist problem in them. But, two hours later, he had learned nothing new, and he left discouraged. He bought himself some lunch and realized he had nothing to do until it was time to get the bus back to Sprocketsville. He wanted to arrive home the same time he usually did so his mother wouldn't ask any questions. He sighed, and wondered if he should go to the matinee of a movie he'd already seen or to the Blitzberg Historical Museum, which he and his classmates had visited on school trips every year since first grade. Without much enthusiasm, he chose the latter.

He was in the Inventions Room examining an odd-looking camera when a voice next to him said, "That camera belonged to Great-Uncle Eustace. He invented it to take pictures underground. If he'd bothered to patent it, he might have made a fortune."

Bart stood there and let out a laugh. I might have known he'd show up here, he thought. "Hello, Arvie," he said, turning toward the shorter boy. "You communing with Great-Uncle Eustace here too?"

"No. Today I'm doing research for a science paper. Mrs. Kresky excused me for the day."

"Yeah?"

"Yes. What paper are you working on?"

"Phys. ed.," Bart said.

"Really? I never heard of a paper for physical education. Don't you have Mr. Dibbetts for a teacher?"

"Yeah."

"That's odd. So do I. He's never asked anyone in my class to do a research paper."

"You've got to get on his good side first," Bart said.

Arvie looked at him with a puzzled expression. Then he said, "Uh, Bart. Your sister, Leanne. How is she?"

"Fine."

"Do you happen to know if she . . . uh . . . enjoyed the book?"

"The book? What book?"

"*Haunted Houses and How to Find Them.* I gave it to her after the dance at Hobby Academy."

"Oh, yeah. She mentioned that. She was very excited about it."

"She was?"

"Sure. She said you were sweet to give it to her."

"Really?"

"Yes, and . . ." Suddenly Bart had an idea. "Hey, Arvie. You don't by any chance have any other books on ghosts or poltergeists, do you?"

"Sure. I've got a whole collection. Some of them are pretty old too; they belonged to Great-Uncle Eustace."

"Yeah? I'd like to take a look at them — for Leanne."

"Okay," Arvie said. "But maybe she'd like

to see them for herself." He promptly turned the color of a pomegranate.

"Uh, no. She's busy. Rehearsing. And anyway, I'd like to surprise her."

"Oh." Arvie looked disappointed. But then he said, "When would you like to come over?"

"How about right now?"

"But your report..."

"I've done enough research for it."

"I haven't. I still..."

"Mrs. Kresky will excuse you for another day. See, I don't have a lot of time, with football and all. Today's really the only day I can do this. For Leanne."

At the mention of her name, Arvie's eyes got fuzzy behind his glasses. "Well, maybe I can spare the time. For Leanne," he said, and led the way out of the museum.

Bart knew he must be really desperate to spend the afternoon at Arvie Biedemeyer's house — and he hoped his sacrifice paid off. Arvie recommended a few books, and Bart picked out a few others. He put them in his backpack and made as quick an exit as he could in order to get home by four o'clock, the time he usually arrived after practice and Yumby's. He didn't want to arouse his mother's suspicions in any way.

As soon as he walked up his driveway, he knew he'd blown it. Mrs. Hawkins was standing with her face pressed against the window, and her expression wasn't one of delight.

Bart frantically tried to come up with a good excuse for why he'd cut school as the front door flung open and his mother rushed out to him.

"Now, Bart. I don't want you to be concerned. It's nothing. Really. I'm sure it isn't. Your father's not worried either."

"What?" Bart said, confused. They walked up the steps.

"We're sure there's a logical explanation — we just have to find it."

"I'm not staying here another minute. I'm not!" Leanne's voice shrieked. She ran out the door.

"Leanne!" Mrs. Hawkins said.

Leanne didn't answer. She just hurtled past them, down the porch steps and out of sight.

"Holy cow! Look at that!" Bart heard Dusty yell. His voice was coming from the living room.

"Look out!" shouted Mr. Hawkins. There was an enormous crash.

"Oh my Lord. It's started again!" Mrs. Hawkins yelled and rushed past him.

Bart flung down his backpack and raced after her. When he got to the living room door, he stood there and gulped.

There was a splintered coffee table sitting in the middle of the room and no other furniture whatsoever. "Where's . . ." he began. Then he noticed his father and brother staring at the ceiling. He looked up too. There was everything else — sofa, chairs, lamps, end tables, TV, bookshelves, grandfather clock — all hanging from the ceiling. Bart let out a sound that was half laugh, half sob.

"There's got to be a logical explanation," Mrs. Hawkins said hysterically. "There's got to be."

"There is, Mom," said Dusty. "We've got ghosts in the house. Right, Bart?"

Bart let out another laugh-sob and sank to the floor in a dead faint.

Chapter 20

Bart slept for thirteen hours straight. He was not aware of his father checking up on him or his mother tucking an extra blanket over his feet. He was also not aware of the discreet calls his parents were placing to find someone to help them clear 1351 Hexum Road of what Mrs. Hawkins was now calling The Problem.

When he finally awoke at five o'clock the next morning, he saw that Millicent was in the room with him.

"Ohhh, what happened to me?" he groaned. "I feel like I've been dead. . . . I mean, excuse me, I . . ."

"You passed out when you discovered that the jig is up."

"Ohhh," Bart groaned. "Stryker."

"Yes. Stryker."

There was a long silence. Then Bart said, "We're in big trouble, aren't we?"

"I'm afraid so," Millicent agreed. "Your parents have set up an appointment for Saturday."

"An appointment with whom?"

"With Operation: Apparition."

"Who?"

"Operation: Apparition, or what you would call ghostbusters."

"Oh no! Saturday! What are we going to do? Isn't there any way you can stop them from discovering you're here?"

"We can lie low, but Stryker? The energy he's putting out could run their machines. He'll certainly be detected. Then they'll eliminate him, and in the process, the rest of us."

"Can't you leave, and come back after the ghostbusters have gotten rid of Stryker?" Bart asked.

"No," answered Millicent. "Once the ghostbusters go to work on one ghost, they make the house uninhabitable for any other ghosts. We could never return again."

Bart sat up. "Look, we can't give up yet. I got some more books from a kid named Arvie Biedemeyer. I didn't get to read them. Maybe they'll have something useful in them." He scrambled out of bed and got his backpack. "Here. I'll read them out loud to you, and you can tell me if anything sounds good."

"All right," Millicent said.

A few hours later, just as dawn was breaking, Bart looked miserably at Millicent hovering next to him. "Nothing," he said.

"Nothing," she agreed. "But don't feel bad, Bart. You've tried to help us. You really have. And we're more than grateful."

Bart said nothing for a moment. Then he

rasped, "I don't want you to be . . . eliminated, Millie. You're . . . special. I can talk to you like I've never talked to anyone else ever before." He reached out to touch her hand, and his fingers passed right through it.

"You mean a lot to me too, Bart," she said softly. There was a strange catch to her voice. Suddenly, she said, "I'm growing tired. I've been visible a long time tonight. It's quite draining. I must go. I'll be back tomorrow."

"Millie . . ." Bart said, but she'd faded away. And he had a distinct feeling she'd left something unsaid.

Bart's parents were so pleased to see him at breakfast they both tried to ignore the pots and pans that were flying around the room, thanks to Stryker's latest burst of mischief. They assured Bart that The Problem would soon be taken care of.

"The ghostbusters are coming," Dusty put in.

"Yeah, I heard," Bart said.

His parents looked a bit puzzled, since they hadn't told him yet, but they didn't say anything.

"Where's Leanne?" he asked.

"She's staying over at Rocky's until The Problem is cleared up," Mrs. Hawkins said.

"She told Rocky we have a poltergeist?"

"Oh, dear me, no. She told her she wasn't getting along with you."

"Oh, great," Bart said sarcastically.

"I understand how you feel, Bart, but we

can't have The Problem spread all over town, can we?"

Bart muttered a response, finished off his oatmeal, and left for school.

He dragged through the day, hardly able to concentrate on a thing.

At lunchtime, Lisa came up to him. "Hello, Bart. I hear you've been sick," she said.

He knew she was giving him the chance to make amends, but he couldn't deal with it. "Yeah," he mumbled and walked away, leaving her standing there in hurt surprise.

When he got to gym class, Coach Dibbetts was overjoyed to see him. Bart could tell because the corners of his mouth twitched up for two seconds. "About time, Hawkins," he said. "I was beginning to think you haven't been eating your Wheaties."

"I'm okay, Coach," he said.

"You better be more than okay, Hawkins. We're taking on the Surgeons in four days."

"Right, Coach," Bart said, thinking, I'll put my mind into practice today and forget about Millicent and the ghostbusters.

But when practice came, Bart couldn't concentrate on it either, and Coach Dibbetts chewed him out hard.

Bart left quickly after practice, avoiding his friends. He was walking down Plunkett Street, his head down, his heart heavy, when he heard someone call, "Bart! Bart Hawkins!" He sighed and turned around.

Arvie Biedemeyer was puffing toward him.

"I . . . I was hoping . . . to run . . . into you," he panted. "I found something last night . . . Leanne might enjoy."

"Yeah?" Bart said without enthusiasm.

"Yes. One of Great-Uncle Eustace's diaries I'd never read before. It chronicles his experiences in a haunted house right in Shamashugee! Leanne will enjoy it tremendously. I know she will. It's much less technical than the one in which Uncle Eustace discusses his ghost changer and . . . say, are you all right? You're looking a bit . . ."

Bart, eyes bugging out, gripped Arvie's shoulders. "The ghost changer! Tell me about it. Quick!"

"Certainly. I believe I mentioned it to you once before. It was designed to alter the personality of an unpleasant ghost into a pleasant one."

"This device—where is it? The Blitzberg Museum?"

"I'm afraid not. It's been lost."

"The plans, then. Where are they? In the diary?"

"No, not in the diary. I fear they've been lost as well. Unless Uncle Eustace hid them somewhere, perhaps in . . ."

"Hurry up!" Bart bellowed. "We have no time to lose!" He grabbed Arvie's arm and began steering him down the street.

"I'm afraid I don't . . . I really . . . where on earth are we going?" Arvie finally got out.

"To Rowan Woods. On the double," said Bart.

Chapter 21

"Wow! How'd you find these?" Arvie yelled, for once sounding like a regular kid.

"I brushed my hand over the fireplace," said Bart pointing to the brass button on the mantel in the cabin. "I pushed it and, presto!"

"Wow!" Arvie said again.

"So, what do you think? These are the plans for the ghost changer, aren't they?"

"Most definitely." Arvie looked up from the papers to Bart and went all professorial again. "I'm indebted to you — and so will the Blitzberg Historical Museum be when I give them these."

"The Blitzberg Museum and I will be even happier when you present them with the actual device."

"What do you mean? The machine was lost. Unless you . . . Good grief! You didn't find . . ."

"No, I didn't."

"Then I don't understand."

"I will explain," said Bart. "Following Great-

Uncle Eustace's careful plans, we — that is, you and I — are going to construct a working model of the ghost changer."

"We are?"

"We are."

Arvie thought about it. "Well. Well. I must say it's an exciting idea. But first of all, these plans may be hard to interpret. . . ."

"You can do it, Arvie. I know you can, with that . . . uh . . . prodigious brain of yours."

"Thank you, but I'm not so certain even *my* brain is prodigious enough. But, assuming it is, there's the second problem of money."

"Money?" Bart looked puzzled.

"For materials — and I'd say, at a quick glance, some of them are far from inexpensive. There's gold filament and some ragatite crystal."

"I've got two hundred and eighty-five bucks in my savings account, plus three hundred in savings bonds. Will that cover it?"

"Five hundred and eighty-five dollars. I should think so, but that's an awful lot of money for you to contribute to such a venture."

"Yeah, well. It's for a good cause. We don't want Uncle Eustace to have died in vain, do we?"

Arvie gave him a bewildered look. "No, I suppose not. But I don't understand why you're so interested in . . ."

Bart cut him off. "You give me the list of stuff we'll need and I'll go buy it."

"You may not be able to find some of these items in Sprocketsville."

"I'll go to Blitzberg then or Shamashugee or all the way to Telva City if I have to. What do you say we get started?"

"You mean you want to work on this today?"

"Sure, today. The faster we get it done, the faster old Eustace will have his . . . uh . . . reputation back."

"I can't possibly start working on this today. I've got to finish off that project for Mrs. Kresky."

"Ask Mrs. Kresky for an extension. She'll give it to you."

"Even if she does, I'm also in the midst of an even more important project that's going to take me another month at least to complete. It's a psychological study of rock musicians. I think *Psychology Today* might be interested in it."

"A month? You mean to tell me some rock musicians you don't even know are more important than your Great-Uncle Eustace?"

Arvie stiffened a little. "It's a significant study."

"How would you like me to arrange a meeting between you and a rock musician to help you along with your study?"

"You could do that?"

"Sure. Easy as pie."

"Who is it? The musician?"

"My sister, Leanne."

"Leanne." As usual, Arvie became lobster colored.

"You think she'd agree to meet with me?"

"Absolutely. I told you — she thinks you're sweet."

Arvie turned even redder. "Okay."

"Great. And in exchange, you and I will start working on this ghost changer right now. So, here's a pen and paper. Make me a list of the supplies we need."

Arvie did. But just as he was about to hand Bart the list, he said, "Wait a minute. Even if we manage to build this, how are we going to test it? Where are we going to find a ghost that needs a personality change?"

"Don't worry about that now. First, let's build this thing." Bart reached for the list, but Arvie was still clutching it.

"No, if we're going to vindicate my Great-Uncle Eustace, we've got to do it properly. It's pointless to build the device unless we can prove that it works. In order to prove it works, we've got to have a ghost, one that's verified as obnoxious by the American Parapsychological Society; and then, when we use the ghost changer, we have to have a witness to verify that the ghost's personality has truly changed. Now, I can easily contact the American Parapsychological Society, but we don't have a ghost — "

"Yes, we do," Bart said.

"Where? Where do we have a ghost?" Arvie asked.

Bart hesitated for a moment; then he said, "In my house."

"What? How long . . . I mean, how do . . . I mean, are you sure?"

"As sure as William Shakespeare wrote *Macbeth*."

Arvie frowned. "It's possible that Christopher Marlowe or Francis Bacon wrote *Macbeth*, or even . . ."

"Stop it!" Bart bellowed.

Arvie did.

After a pause, Bart said in a quieter voice, "There is a nasty poltergeist at 1351 Hexum Road, and not only I, but my whole family, has seen him in action. He's wrecking our house and our nerves, and if we don't do something about him soon, we're all going to go nuts. Now do you believe me?"

Arvie nodded slowly. Then he asked, "But why do you want to change his personality? Why don't you just want to get rid of him?"

Bart hesitated again. Then, with a sigh, he said, "Okay. I guess I've got to trust someone — and it might as well be you." And Bart proceeded to tell him the whole story.

Chapter 22

"Move that transcendentor to the right. Yes, that's it. Now take the turwilliger pin and put it next to the ragatite crystal," Arvie instructed Bart.

"Are you sure that's where it goes? I thought that's where we put it last time — just before we shorted out half your house," Bart responded.

"No, no. That time we had the turwilliger pin next to the herminutor. And that isn't why we shorted out anyway. We shorted out because we overloaded the coils."

"The coils? You can't overload the coils."

"Yes, you can and we did."

"You're crazy, Arvie. You can overload circuits, but not coils."

Arvie gave Bart a long-suffering look and said, "Instead of arguing with me, Bart, will you please put the turwilliger pin next to the ragatite crystal?"

"Yes, master," Bart said.

He and Arvie had been working feverishly all week on the ghost changer in the Biedemeyers' basement. Bart was better with his hands, so he'd done most of the building. Arvie was better at explaining what had to be done, so he got to give directions. They'd both run into some big snags — deciphering Uncle Eustace's spidery scrawl hadn't been easy, and finding the right-shaped crystal did take Bart all the way to Telva City. But the device was definitely taking shape. In fact, it was almost finished — and that was a good thing, because the ghostbusters were coming the very next day, right after the big game against the Surgeons.

The plan was for Bart to give Arvie a spare key, so he could let himself and the members of the American Parapsychological Society he'd contacted into the house while Bart and his family were at the game. The parapsychologists could observe the poltergeist for at least two hours — and then Arvie would use the ghost changer, and they'd document the results.

Bart was sorry that he wasn't going to be there himself to see Stryker undergo his personality change, but there was no other safe way to execute their plan.

"Okay, the turwilliger pin is next to the ragatite crystal," he said. "What next?"

"Let me see . . . I believe . . . yes, that's it."

"Yes, what's it?"

"We're finished. It's done."

Bart's eyes widened. "It is? Are you sure?"

"I'm as sure as the fact that William Shakespeare wrote *Macbeth*," Arvie said.

"But you told me William Shakespeare might not have . . ." Bart began. Then he looked at Arvie and realized that for the first time he was making a joke.

"We did it!" Bart yelled. "We did it!" He jumped up and grabbed Arvie in a bear hug.

"Too bad there's no way of testing it before tomorrow," Arvie said when Bart let him go.

"Why do you say that?" Bart asked, his brow furrowing. "It'll work, won't it? It's got to."

"It should — we followed Uncle Eustace's notes to the letter."

"Then there's nothing to worry about," Bart said, and slapping the spare key into Arvie's palm, he left — and worried all the way home.

"This is the third time this week you've been late for dinner," his mother chided when he got there.

"I'm sorry, Mom," Bart said, sitting down to cold meat loaf. He hated upsetting her. But some things were more important than his mother's feelings or cold meat loaf or even football. He'd been really lousy in practice all week. So lousy that Coach Dibbetts had stopped chewing him out — always a bad sign — and his teammates were beginning to talk behind his back. But his mind was full of the ghost changer — something he couldn't tell the coach, his teammates, or anyone else, except Millie.

"What have you been up to after school anyway?" his mother said. "I ran into Lisa today. She said she hadn't seen you much lately. She seemed upset. Have you two broken up?"

"Uh, sort of," Bart said, and then realized it was true. They had broken up — or slid apart, as it were — hadn't they?

"And Greg called just before to talk with you. He seemed surprised that you weren't home, because he said he hasn't seen you at Yumby's for a while. So what have you been up to?"

"I've been working on . . . uh . . . a science project."

"With whom?"

"With whom?" Bart repeated.

"Yes. Since you're not working on it here, you must be working on it at someone else's house."

"Uh . . . yeah. I've been working on it with . . ."

"Arvie Biedemeyer," said Leanne as she came into the kitchen.

"How did you know that?" Bart blurted out. "You don't even know Arvie Biedemeyer." At least you don't know you do, he thought.

"I heard two kids talking about you at Tops and Bottoms. One said, and I quote, 'Can you believe it? Kristi saw it with her own eyes. Bart Hawkins coming out of Arvie Biedemeyer's house — and not once, but twice. What's the Hawk doing with that nerd?' Then the other one said, 'I don't know, but I heard that Bart and Lisa broke up because Bart's been acting weird.' "

"That's quite enough, Leanne," Mrs. Hawkins said sharply.

Leanne shut up, but she kept a smug smile on her face.

Bart turned his head so he wouldn't have to look at her. It had happened. Everything he was afraid would happen. His love life, his rep — ruined, all ruined. He left his plate untouched and went to his room. "Bart the Bald," he said, staring into his mirror. "Found me out. Bart the Bald."

Chapter 23

"Way to play, Hawkins," Coach Dibbetts said, slapping Bart on the butt.

The third quarter of the game had just ended, and the Phantoms were leading the Shamashugee Surgeons twenty to fourteen. Both teams had been playing hard and well — and the game was far from over, even though there was only one quarter to go.

Through a supreme effort of will, Bart had managed to put all his concentration into the game. Everything else was in Arvie's hands — Arvie's and Great-Uncle Eustace's. There was nothing at this point he could do for Millie and her friends. Right now he had another job — to be the Phantoms' star quarterback and blunt the Surgeons' nasty scalpels.

The fourth quarter began. The Phantoms had possession of the ball. Bart and his teammates got into a huddle.

"Mash forty-one on two," Bart said.

"Mash forty-one?" said Tony Martini. "You sure?"

Bart gave him a look that silenced him at once. Then he said, "Okay. Break!"

He and his teammates got into position, facing the Surgeons on their own thirty-eight-yard line.

"Twenty-nine, fifty-three, twenty-five. *Hut* one! *Hut* two!" Bart got the snap, handed the ball to Tony, and faked a handoff to the fullback, who ran past the right end. The halfback ran through a hole between the center and the guard for a gain of twelve yards.

"All right!" Greg cheered.

"Let's hear it for the Hawk! He'll make the Surgeons squawk!" the cheerleaders cheered.

Bart heard the chant and grinned. Maybe he wasn't about to become heavyweight contender for school nerd after all. He turned to wink at Lisa. As he did, he noticed some sort of fracas in the stands. It looked as though a kid had tripped over someone else in the bleachers. The trippee was being hauled to his feet by a big bruiser twice his size. Suddenly Bart blinked. He was pretty far away from the stands, but even from that distance he could tell that the little kid was Arvie Biedemeyer.

Oh no. Something's gone wrong. He wasn't supposed to come to the game, he thought, feeling himself get frantic. Hold on, hold on. Maybe the ghost changer worked like a charm, and he just came to watch the Phantoms win the game, a calmer voice said. Watch the Phantoms win?

172

Arvie Biedemeyer doesn't care a fig about football. No, something's definitely gone wrong.

"Hey, Bart. We know Lisa's got great legs, but you can look at 'em later," Frankie LaRocha, a tackle, said.

"Yeah, Hawk. Time to give us the play," said Bob Lucas.

"Uh, right."

They went into another huddle. "Uh. Twenty-five flare," Bart said. "On three."

"Twenty-five flare?" Tony said.

Bart gave him another look, but this time Tony kept talking. "That couldn't be right," he said.

A couple of other players mumbled in agreement.

Bart ignored them. "Okay, break!" he commanded, but he noticed just before they got into position that Greg was giving him a puzzled look.

"Forty-six, ninety-seven, eleven. *Hut* one! *Hut* two! *Hut* three!" he called. He got the snap and threw a long pass to Greg. But just before the ball reached him, the pass was intercepted by the Surgeons' free safety.

No one said anything to Bart as they switched positions from offense to defense. On defense, Bart played safety. He took his place in the backfield. What had gone wrong? he worried. Why would Arvie come to the game? The machine must've failed. But if that was it, why . . .

". . . *hut* four!" The Surgeons' center snapped

the ball to their quarterback. He didn't have it. Someone else did. Who was it? The fullback. He was running, running right past the Phantoms' linebackers. Why wasn't anyone stopping him? He was going to get a touchdown. Bart charged at the fullback, reached for him, and got a handful of face mask as he pulled him down.

Wheet! The referee blew his whistle. "Personal foul! Face-masking. Fifteen-yard penalty."

There were assorted hisses and boos from the crowd.

The Surgeons lined up again. "Eighteen, sixteen, fifty-four, sixty-two. *Hut* one!" This time their quarterback faked a handoff to the halfback and ran the ball himself to the Phantoms' end zone for a touchdown, tying the score twenty to twenty.

There was a hush as the kicker kicked for the point after. He made it. The Surgeons were ahead.

Kickoff, and the Phantoms once again got the ball on their twenty-yard line.

"Swing pass on four," Bart said.

"All right!" said Greg.

Break. Positions. Down. "Nineteen, fifteen, fifty-one. *Hut* one! *Hut* two! *Hut* three! *Hut* four!" Bart, ball in hand, faded back. He cocked his arm. Bloop! The ball slipped out of his hand and was pounced on by the Surgeons.

Bart bit his lip. He felt terribly embarrassed. Like every other player, he'd fumbled the ball on occasion. But never so clumsily. Time was going fast. The Phantoms would need every bit of skill — and luck — they had or could get to pull this one out of the fire.

They didn't have enough of either. The Surgeons won — by a single point. Heads lowered in defeat, the Phantoms slumped off the field. This time, Bart's teammates scarcely said a word. Bart figured that Coach Dibbetts would have plenty to say, but instead the coach just told them he'd see them all Monday at practice.

Bart showered quickly and rushed out. He wasn't in a hurry to see his family. It was Arvie he was anxious to talk with.

But his family found him first. Mr. Hawkins was a lot more talkative than the coach — full of criticism and advice. But Bart barely heard what he said. He was looking for Arvie. Finally he spotted a round, freckled face coming his way.

"Excuse me, Dad," Bart said and ran over to him. "Arvie! What's wrong? What are you doing here? Didn't it work?"

"Well, uh, not exactly."

"What do you mean, not exactly?"

"Well, Mr. Smithers and Miss Durocher of the American Parapsychological Society showed up right on time and I let us in with the key you gave me. They set up their equipment, but it was hardly necessary because your poltergeist put on quite a show. It was really astounding. At one point, the entire carpet rolled up right to our feet, and the sofa . . ."

"I've seen Stryker in action. What happened with the ghost changer?"

"Well, after monitoring the poltergeist's activity for a while, we felt it was time to use it. I worked the controls. It was amazing. The ghost's activity ceased at once. The meter registered a positive energy output. Mr. Smithers and Miss Durocher were quite impressed. They pronounced Uncle Eustace's invention worthy of increased study. Then the machine, along with several pieces of furniture, flew across the room, striking Mr. Smithers in the head. The machine did that, not the furniture. I took the liberty of using your phone to call an ambulance, which arrived quite promptly, but proved to be unnecessary, since Mr. Smithers had recovered quickly from the blow and asked Miss Durocher to drive him home."

"Oh, jeez," Bart said, closing his eyes.

"Er . . . I was able to rescue the device. I don't think it was badly damaged. I can't imagine why it didn't work. And I'm afraid it rather enraged your poltergeist. He wreaked quite a bit of havoc with several cans of paint. Fortunately, that was only in one room."

"Which room was it?" Bart asked in a daze, his eyes still shut.

"Er . . . I'm not certain," said Arvie. "But from the furnishings, I'd hazard a guess that it was yours."

Chapter 24

Bart stood in his wrecked room and blinked back tears. There were streaks of red paint slashed across the walls, the floor, the ceiling, the bed, and the mirror. His closet door had been wrenched out and lay on the floor, and his clothes were spattered with green paint. All of the books on his shelf were painted black. That was all bad enough, but what was really hurting him the most was the fact that he'd truly and utterly failed.

"Can I come in?" Dusty asked from the doorway.

Bart, unable to speak, nodded.

His brother entered cautiously, surveying the damage. Then he laid his hand on Bart's arm. "The ghost did it, didn't he?"

Bart nodded again.

"Don't worry. He'll be gone soon. The ghostbusters will take care of him."

That was when Bart put his hands over his eyes and started to cry.

* * *

Some time later, his parents called him downstairs alone for a talk.

"Bart, we've just had a phone call from Mr. Rollins," his mother said. "He claims that he saw an ambulance pull up in front of our house at around three-thirty this afternoon. But it left without a passenger. However, a short time later, Mr. Rollins saw three people come out of our house — a woman, a man with a cut on his forehead, and a boy carrying a black box. From the description Mr. Rollins gave us, we would say the boy is the same one who showed up after your game today: Arvie Biedemeyer. We know he didn't sneak into our house because Mr. Rollins saw him lock the door with a key. So the question is, Bart, what the devil is going on?"

Bart looked down at his hands. They didn't seem to belong to him. Nothing seemed to belong to him. "I gave Arvie a spare key," he said.

"Why?"

"To let himself and the two members of the American Parapsychological Society in."

"The American Parapsychological Society? Are they like the ghostbusters?" Mr. Hawkins asked.

Bart shook his head. "No. They don't get rid of ghosts. They just study them."

"Why did you let them in without asking us?" Mrs. Hawkins questioned.

"We wanted to try out our ghost . . ." He

paused. It was silly. The machine hadn't worked, but he still felt the need to protect it. "Detector," he finished.

"The black box," Mr. Hawkins said.

"The science project you and Arvie were working on," said Mrs. Hawkins.

"Yes. To detect ghosts."

"Nobody needs a machine to detect this ghost," Mr. Hawkins said.

"Uh . . . well . . . anyway, I didn't tell you because I knew you didn't want anyone else to know about the ghost, and I thought you'd be upset if you found out Arvie and the American Parapsychological Society knew. I'm sorry."

"I suspect the American Parapsychological Society is even sorrier," Mrs. Hawkins said dryly.

"Yeah. Arvie said Stry . . . I mean, the poltergeist threw our machine at one of them."

"We've got to get rid of the creep," said Mr. Hawkins.

"Yes," agreed his wife. "Speaking of which, where is Operation: Apparition? They were due here at . . ."

She was interrupted by the phone. She picked up the receiver. "Hello, Hawkins residence. Yes . . . yes . . . Oh no. But you *must* come today. It's urgent. The poltergeist wrecked my son's . . . A fire? I agree. Well, that does sound more pressing. But . . ." She sighed. "Well, then, when can you come? Monday morning? But that's two days from now. Yes. Yes, I understand. But . . . but . . . all right." She hung up. "Ratatouille!

They're stuck on a case over in Folger. A ghost that's been committing arson. Oh, Howard, none of us can spend the rest of the weekend here with that thing on the loose. We . . ."

The phone rang again. Mrs. Hawkins picked it up. "Hello, Hawkins residence. Oh, hello, Mother. I'm sorry to hear that. Why yes, as a matter of fact I think we can . . . in about half an hour . . . Good-bye." She hung up. "All right, we're all going to Grandma and Grandpa Beamer's. Everyone get your things together."

Bart didn't bother to protest. A beaten man, he slowly went upstairs to his room to do his mother's bidding, even though he had no un-painted clothes to pack.

On Sunday night, the Hawkinses returned to their house. Bart was offered a new bedroom, but he refused. He just changed the sheets and blankets on his bed, sat down, and waited. It was going to be the last time he ever saw Millie, and he thought that he finally understood what it felt like to be brokenhearted.

She arrived shortly after eleven. "How's your Grandma?" she asked. "Are her nerves any better?"

"Not really," Bart said.

"My grandmother used to have the vapors all the time too until she started taking valerian mixed with chamomile and scullcap. Very sooth-ing. Perhaps your grandmother ought to try that. . . ."

"Millie!" Bart burst out. "I'm never going to

see you again after tonight, and you're talking as though everything's normal."

Millie stopped speaking. Finally, after a long pause, she said, "I'm sorry, Bart. But I'm very bad at good-byes. I always was. Even when I died. My last words weren't 'Farewell' or 'Parting is such sweet sorrow.' They were 'I think this nightgown shrank in the wash.' Anyway, I've been thinking that perhaps it's best that I'll be . . . departing."

"Best? What do mean, best? I told you that you're special to me and you said I mean a lot to you too. What could be good about your going away?"

"Bart, you do mean a lot to me. That's why I ought to go. You've dropped your friends, sacrificed your football playing, and upset your mental and physical health because of me. It isn't right."

"Why not?" Bart asked stubbornly.

"Because I'm a ghost. You mustn't get too attached to a ghost."

Before Bart had a chance to respond, there was a rattle of stones against the window.

"What the heck is that?" he said, jumping up. He opened the window and stuck his head out. In the moonlight, he could just make out a short, pudgy form on the grass below. "Arvie?" he asked.

"Oh, thank goodness I got the right room. Can you let me in?"

"Shh. Lower your voice. I'll be right down." He turned to Millicent. "I don't know what's going on, but it probably won't take long. Will you . . ."

"I'll wait," she answered.

Bart rushed out of his room and down the stairs as quickly and quietly as he could. He unlocked the front door and padded out on the porch. "What the heck are you doing here at this hour?" he asked. "My parents know you were here yesterday. I had to tell them . . ."

"The ghostbusters. Have they come yet?" Arvie cut in.

"No. They had to postpone their visit. They're coming tomorrow instead."

"Excellent. Then there's still time."

"What are you talking about?"

"The ghost changer. I was going over the notes. And I think I know where we went wrong."

"You do?"

"Yes. The only problem is it has to do with one of the formulas. My math is only adequate. We could easily go wrong again — unless you happen to be better at math than I am."

"Me? Nah. I don't know that kind of math at all."

"Oh." Arvie's face fell.

But Bart's lit up. "On the other hand, I know someone who might."

"You do? Can we reach him now? I know it's late, but . . ."

"Yeah, I think we can get hold of him, considering that he's right upstairs."

"Your father? I thought . . ."

"No, not my father. My brother, Dusty."

"If there's a vector . . ." Dusty lowered his head to the paper and snored. It was the third time he'd fallen asleep while trying to figure out the formula.

"Come on, Dusty. Wake up," Bart nudged him.

Dusty's eyes shot open. "Uh . . . where am I?"

"At home in the rec room, trying to help Arvie and me with a matter of life and death."

"How am I supposed to get this right when you won't tell me what it's about?" the math genius whined, sounding exactly like an eleven-year-old kid.

"Once you work it out, we'll tell you what it's for. But if we tell you first, it will only distract you," Arvie explained patiently.

Bart had always thought of himself as a patient person, but next to Arvie, he had the fidgets. It annoyed him to discover that. "How come you're willing to work on this?" he whispered irritably. "You don't think the American Parapsychological Society would be dumb enough to come here again — even if there was time for them to. So your Uncle Eustace's name will still be mud. And as for my darling sister . . ." He stopped before he went too far.

Arvie looked at him calmly and whispered back, "Yes, I know the A.P.S. won't respond to a second call. As for Leanne, I am looking forward to the meeting with her you agreed to arrange. But surely you must see that it would be a shame — a *crime* — to leave this project incomplete, the A.P.S. notwithstanding. That's how Uncle Eustace would have felt too." He paused, then continued. "There's another reason I'm working on this too."

"What is it?" Bart asked reluctantly. He was already feeling embarrassed at his outburst, especially since they had so little time to waste.

Arvie reddened. "I enjoy your company."

"You do?"

"Yes. I don't have any other friends — and I think for a football player you're an okay guy."

Now Bart was really ashamed. He knew he'd taken advantage of Arvie. The kid was a nerd, that was true. But for a nerd, he was kind of okay. "I . . . I'm sorry," Bart started to say. Then he heard a sound above him. He looked up at the ceiling. "What's that?"

They listened quietly.

"Footsteps!" said Bart. "Quick, put out the light!"

Arvie reached for the lamp and knocked it over. Bart caught it just before it hit the floor, and flicked the switch.

They heard the rec room door open and they froze — except for Dusty, who let out a big yawn. Bart clapped his hand over his brother's mouth.

They sat perfectly still for what seemed like an hour. Then, the rec room door closed. But they didn't move until they heard the footsteps retreat. Then Bart let out a sigh of relief, flicked on the light again, and turned to Dusty. "Okay, back to work," he said.

But Dusty had fallen asleep once more.

An hour later, Dusty, whom Bart had had to wake up four more times, said, "Okay, I think this is it." He explained the formula.

Bart didn't understand a thing he was saying, but Arvie nodded. "So we move the angle of the deflector two degrees rather than fifteen degrees?" Arvie asked.

"Yes. That's right."

"That means we have to reset the vibration meter too. No wonder it didn't work right."

"Okay. You promised to tell me what this is about," Dusty said.

Arvie nodded again. He lifted up the ghost changer from behind the sofa and put it on the Ping-Pong table. Prying off the lid, he readjusted the deflector and reset the meter.

"That's all it needed?" Bart asked.

"If Dusty and I are right, that's all," Arvie said.

"Okay. Then let's try it. We have no time to lose."

All of a sudden the room was filled with icy cold.

The ghost changer began to slide across the table, scattering balls and Ping-Pong paddles as it did. Arvie made a grab for it, tripped, and fell.

Bart was quicker. He sprawled across the

table and got both arms around the box. "It's okay," he said to Arvie and Dusty. But it wasn't. In another moment, he and the table began to slide across the room.

"Press the lever on the left," Arvie ordered.

Bart tried, but he found he couldn't move his fingers. The table gathered speed and crashed into the wall, throwing Bart and the box to the floor.

"Bart!" Dusty screamed.

"The lever!" yelled Arvie.

Shaken, but unhurt, Bart got to his knees. He was still clutching the ghost changer, but his fingers were frozen in place.

Arvie tried to run toward him and was knocked flat. Dusty got a few steps farther before the sofa and two chairs soared forward, imprisoning his legs between them.

"Stryker, you maniac!" Bart shouted. With a supreme effort, he inched his fingers forward toward the little silver lever. "Owww!" he yelled. His fingers stung from an unseen slap. His head jerked back. The poltergeist was pulling his hair.

"Now press the red button," Arvie yelled. "That polarizes . . ."

"I know, I know. I built this . . . owww!" Bart hollered. Stryker had struck his hand again. The single light in the room went out and something (a Ping-Pong paddle?) flew across the room and struck him in the shins. Something else (the bar?) thundered past him. Bart felt the ghost changer slipping out of his grasp. He didn't know how he'd managed to hold on to it all this time.

Suddenly, a deep bass voice cried, "Stryker!" And in the right-hand corner of the room, a ball of silver appeared, stretching into the lanky form of a middle-aged man. In the left-hand corner, two higher male voices repeated the cry. Bart turned his head and saw another ball of silver split in two and shape into twin boys, eighteen years old or so.

"Stupendous!" said Arvie.

"Mommy," whispered Dusty.

Bart said nothing. A fourth ghost, female, materialized in front of him. Then a fifth. All around him, the ghosts appeared, calling Stryker's name over and over. An elderly gentleman. Old Man Koral, Bart guessed. A sad-looking woman in her twenties. Lydia. A woman of some thirty-five years in a flashy dress. Lurlene, probably. What were they doing? Millie said they couldn't overpower the poltergeist. Then Millie herself appeared. And Bart understood. No, they can't overpower him, but they can distract him. He realized he could move his hands again. Without wasting any more time, he felt for the polarizer button and pushed it.

"No!" another voice rose above the others. The ceiling shook with the sound. "No! No! No!"

Bart pushed the button again. The ghost changer made a *ssst* sound and a small beam of green light shot out from its side.

"No! N . . ." the voice wailed, then died.

The room went silent. The ceiling stopped shaking. The furniture stopped moving. The ghosts stopped calling and wavered without a word in their places. Bart didn't dare speak.

Then Old Man Koral came forward slowly. He stretched out his hand and pinched at the air.

"Ouch!" a small, high-pitched voice whined.

A flicker of light, and a tenth ghost appeared at the elderly apparition's side. A short, scawny ghost with long hair, a poor-boy cap, and knickers, his ear firmly in the grip of Old Man Koral's thumb and forefinger.

"Who's that?" said Bart. "That's not . . ."

"Yes. It is," said Old Man Koral. "The obnoxious little bugger himself." He gave the poltergeist a shake. "Now, my lad. What do you have to say for yourself?" He pushed the poltergeist forward.

The small ghost looked at Bart, gave a sheepish smile, and said, "I've been rather a beastly little fellow, haven't I?"

Chapter 25

"Okay, guys. Now listen and listen good," Coach Dibbetts said. "You all know nothing much is riding on this game — just a little thing called the league championship, that's all. So I'm asking you to do something you haven't done for a while: *Win!* Everybody got that? Good. Hawkins!"

"Yeah, Coach," Bart answered crisply.

"You screwed up the last two games."

"I know I did, Coach."

"But considering you looked okay in practice this week, I'm going to make the assumption that you still know how to play this game. And you darn well better not prove me wrong, or I'll kick your asterisk between the goalposts."

"I will . . . I mean, I won't, Coach," Bart said. He was glad that Dibbetts was chewing him out again instead of giving him the silent treatment.

He was happy about something else too. Millie and her friends were really and truly safe. When the ghostbusters came on Monday, they found no evidence of any ghosts whatsoever — even though they spent the entire day in the Hawkinses' house. Bart's parents were pretty upset. "Why, just last night that thing made a huge mess of our rec room," Mrs. Hawkins told them. She and Mr. Hawkins had gotten downstairs just after the ghosts had faded away with Stryker in tow. Bart, Arvie, and Dusty had hidden in the boiler room and fortunately were not discovered.

"Well, perhaps that was his last gasp," one of the ghostbusters said, "because you certainly don't have any poltergeist now."

Bart's folks had rather a bad week after that, expecting The Problem to resurface any minute. But when it didn't, they decided the ghostbusters must've been right, and neither Bart nor Dusty, who was sworn to secrecy, bothered to correct them.

Since Bart had succeeded after all in helping the ghosts, today Millie and her friends were going to keep their part of the bargain. Bart's conscience was bothering him. But he still wanted the Phantoms to win. Nobody will know about the ghosts. Not even the Phantoms. And, ghosts or not, we're all going to play as hard and smart as we can, he thought, trying to convince his conscience to pipe down.

"Okay." Coach Dibbetts was finishing his pep talk. "Now get the heck out there and slice up the Surgeons!"

"All right!" everyone cheered.

"Who's gonna win?" yelled Tony Martini.

"The Phantoms!" everyone yelled back.

With a little help from some other phantoms, Bart added silently, and ran out onto the field with the rest of his team.

A roar went up from the huge crowd. The stands were filled to overflowing, spilling people out along the sidelines, even into neighboring trees — and all because the Hawk was playing. Bart heard and saw them, and flashed a king-sized smile that made them all roar louder.

The referee held up the coin. "Heads," the Surgeons' quarterback called. The referee tossed the coin.

"Heads," he said.

"We elect to receive," the Surgeons' quarterback said.

"Okay, Bob, give it a good boot — far, but not too far," Bart's teammates called.

Bob put the ball on the tee on the Phantoms' forty-yard line. He took five steps back, turned, and faced the ball. The referee blew the whistle. Bob ran toward the ball and kicked. The ball arced high across the field.

Darn, thought Bart. It's going to land in the end zone.

But suddenly the ball did a nosedive and dropped like a stone — right on the Surgeons' one-yard line. The Surgeons' right end smothered it and was, in turn, smothered.

"Wow!" "Holy smoke!" "Gee whiz!" the crowd gasped.

Both the Surgeons and the Phantoms were too stunned to speak.

They lined up. The Surgeons' quarterback, Jerry Lamar, got the snap, stepped back to pass the ball, and was promptly sacked in his own end zone by the Phantoms' left tackle, Frankie LaRocha.

"Safety!" the referee announced.

Two points went up for the Phantoms on the scoreboard.

Bart giggled. This is going to be some game, he said to himself.

He was right. The Phantoms played like, well, magic. In the first quarter, they scored a touchdown and extra point. In the second quarter, the Surgeons couldn't even get a first down. The quarterback threw a bomb to number eighty-six, one of his wide receivers, who reached up to catch the ball but slipped instead and fell flat on his face.

Greg Spinetti caught the pass instead.

"Interference!" the Surgeons' receiver yelled, fists clenched, as he got to his feet. "Somebody tripped me!"

"Nobody tripped you," Greg said.

"Oh, yeah?" He went for Greg.

But the referee was there first. "Nobody tripped you," he said. "Get into line or you're out of the game."

The receiver sneered at Greg, but obeyed.

So the Phantoms had the ball again, and it wasn't long before they had their second touchdown on a spectacular play by Tony Martini. The point after was good again.

Halftime. While the band and majorettes put

on a show, the Phantoms sat in the locker room talking about the game.

"That kick — amazing," Greg said.

"That interception — great," said Bob.

"We're playing like we've got angels on our side," said Tom Brewster.

"Well, whatever we've got, tell it, or them, to stick around," said Coach Dibbetts.

"Don't worry, Coach," Bart said confidently. "It — or they — will."

The game resumed. But now the Surgeons retaliated. Touchdown one, on a brilliant pass by Jerry Lamar. Touchdown two, after a bad fumble by the Phantoms' fullback. Two points after, plus a field goal.

So the score was seventeen to sixteen in the fourth quarter, with ten seconds left to play, and the Surgeons were once again threatening to lick the Phantoms by one lousy point.

Millie? Duane and Blaine? Matthias? Hey, what's going on, Bart asked silently. I thought you guys could beat anyone but the '67 Packers. Then another voice in his head said, Forget them, Bart. You're the quarterback of this team. It's up to you and the Phantoms to win — not a team of ghosts.

The Phantoms got into a huddle. Bart looked at the field. Fourth down and six to go on the Surgeons' twenty-three-yard line. Should they try a field goal? No. He thought for another moment. Then he said, "Okay, we're going to try the halfback pass. Got it, Tony?"

"No," Tony said. "I think that's a lousy play."

"Your opinion is noted," Bart said coolly. "The play is halfback pass on two."

"That's what you get from a quarterback who hangs out with Arvie Biedemeyer," Tony muttered.

Some of the Phantoms laughed.

"Shut up, Martini," Greg said, "or instead of running back we'll call you running mouth."

More guys laughed.

Bart shut them all up. "The name of this game is football. Play it, or get off the field." He looked straight at Tony.

No one said a word.

Still looking at Tony, Bart repeated the play once more and commanded, "Break!"

The Phantoms broke and lined up for scrimmage.

"Down!" Bart called. "Eighty-two! Fifty-nine! One hundred and two! *Hut* one! *Hut* two!"

He got the snap, pitched a lateral to Tony, who ran around Tom Brewster. Bart ran the other way, down the left sideline.

The Surgeons ignored him and plunged after Tony. The halfback swiveled to the right, then pivoted and threw the ball toward Bart. It was too high. Bart knew it as he stretched up his arms. Damn, he thought.

Then suddenly, miraculously, he rose into the air, one, two, three feet off the ground. He caught the ball on the two-yard line and took a flying leap backward into the Surgeons' end zone.

Touchdown! Then, *wheet!* The game was over
— the Phantoms had won!

The crowd went wild.

Dazed and overjoyed, Bart was hoisted up on
Frankie LaRocha's and Butch Macrae's shoulders and carried off the field. The two tackles
didn't set him down until they reached the door
to the locker room. All around him people were
cheering, shouting, hugging, and punching each
other with glee. Greg did a somersault. Two
cheerleaders did handsprings.

Bart pulled off his helmet and tossed it in the
air. Someone poured a cup of water over his
head. He shook it, slicked back his hair — his
thick hair — and laughed.

Some girls behind him screamed ecstatically.
He turned around and saw that one of them
was Lisa.

"Oh, Bart!" she said with a smile and hugged
him.

He hugged her back.

When they broke apart, she was still smiling,
but warily.

He started to say something, looked over her
head, and saw Arvie Biedemeyer coming toward
him with a camera.

"Hey, Arvie!" he said loudly and clearly.
"Just the man I wanted to see."

A few heads turned to look at them and
registered a variety of responses, from amused
to shocked to unconcerned.

"Hold it," Arvie said, snapping a photo of
Bart and Lisa.

"What's that for?" Bart asked.

"Assignment," Arvie said. "For *DeForest News and Views.*"

"When did you start working for the paper?"

"Yesterday. I decided it was time to broaden my horizons and show some school spirit. The editor of the paper was delighted — particularly since her photographer had just quit due to an unfortunate accident with a tripod. So I got his job."

"Great!" Bart said. "I've got some good news for you. I was going to call you later to tell you. Leanne's agreed to the da — uh, interview. Tomorrow, two o'clock at Yumby's."

"Really?"

"Really." Bart didn't find it necessary to mention just how he'd gotten Leanne to agree to the date — by telling her her secret admirer was dying to meet her. He hadn't had to demand repayment for the broken dishes coverup and was happy about that. He might need to remind her of that after the date.

"Thanks a lot," Arvie said, and, red as a fire engine, hurried off to finish his assignment.

"So you've decided to help out Arvie after all," Lisa said.

Bart looked at her and said matter-of-factly, "No. Arvie helped me."

Lisa looked puzzled, so Bart continued. "I want to talk with you, Lisa. I want to tell you a few things about Bartholomew Hawkins."

"Okay," she answered slowly. "When?"

"How about as soon as I take a shower?" Bart said with a smile.

"I'll see if I can wait that long," Lisa said. This time her smile wasn't wary at all.

Bart had put on a suit and was just tying his tie when Millicent's voice said, "Oh, Bart. I'm so glad to see you. I've been meaning to apologize . . ."

Bart whirled around. "Millie! Millie! Boy, am I glad to see you too. You were great! Just great! All of you. . . . We should have a victory celebration. Not tonight though, because I'm taking Lisa to the — would you believe — opera. They're doing *Macbeth* over in Blitzberg. Isn't that funny? I don't even know if I like opera. Neither does Lisa. But we were talking today, and we decided it wouldn't hurt to . . . broaden our horizons. Anyway, at least I know the story, so I . . . apologize for what?"

"Did you say that you won today?"

"Of course we won. You know that."

"Oh, I'm so glad. I was so upset. We all were."

"Millie, what the heck are you talking about?"

"The game. You said it was at the high school. So we went there — well, at least we thought we were going there. But instead of a school we found a shopping mall. Then we figured it out — the old school must've been torn down since we died. But none of us knew where the new school was. We spent ages traveling around town trying to find it, with no luck."

"Huh? You mean you never made the game?"

"That's right."

"But Bob's kick with the ball dropping right on the Surgeons' one-yard line, and the way the Surgeons' fullback tripped, and that jump I made to catch Tony's pass . . . You didn't . . . You weren't . . . You mean, that wasn't you — it was us?"

"Yes. And I apologize. Are you terribly angry?"

Bart began to giggle. "Angry? Millie, you just . . . made my . . . day." Then he laughed so hard, she had to join in.

When they finally stopped, she said, "Well, I'm so pleased that your team won and that you're not angry at us. But we still haven't kept our part of the bargain, and that isn't fair. What else can we do for you to show our appreciation?"

"Aww, Millie. You've already done plenty for me," Bart said. He picked up his copy of *Macbeth*, which had survived Stryker's painting fit, and stuck it in his pocket. He peered at himself in the mirror, straightened his collar, then turned back to Millicent. "On the other hand," he kidded, "the basketball season starts next week. You and your friends wouldn't happen to be any good on the court, would you?"

Millicent cocked her head. "Just a moment," she said and disappeared.

"Hey, wait. I was only . . ." Bart began.

But before he could finish, she was back. "Grace says we can beat any team in this country — past or present — except for the 1973 New York Knicks."

"Then Millie, old girl," Bart said with a laugh, "I think I just might know of a way for you and your friends to hold up your end of the deal."

Other books you will enjoy,
about real kids like you!

❏ MZ43124-2	**A Band of Angels** Julian F. Thompson	$2.95
❏ MZ40515-2	**City Light** Harry Mazer	$2.75
❏ MZ40943-3	**Fallen Angels** Walter Dean Myers	$3.50
❏ MZ40428-8	**I Never Asked You to Understand Me** Barthe DeClements	$2.75
❏ MZ43999-5	**Just a Summer Romance** Ann M. Martin	$2.75
❏ MZ44629-0	**Last Dance** Caroline B. Cooney	$2.95
❏ MZ44628-2	**Life Without Friends** Ellen Emerson White	$2.95
❏ MZ43821-2	**A Royal Pain** Ellen Conford	$2.95
❏ MZ44626-6	**Saturday Night** Caroline B. Cooney	$2.95
❏ MZ44429-8	**A Semester in the Life of a Garbage Bag** Gordon Korman	$2.95
❏ MZ44770-X	**Seventeen and In-Between** Barthe DeClement	$2.75
❏ MZ41823-8	**Simon Pure** Julian F. Thompson	$3.50
❏ MZ41838-6	**Slam Book** Ann M. Martin	$2.75
❏ MZ43867-0	**Son of Interflux** Gordon Korman	$2.95
❏ MZ43817-4	**Three Sisters** Norma Fox Mazer	$2.95
❏ MZ41513-1	**The Tricksters** Margaret Mahy	$2.95
❏ MZ44773-3	**When the Phone Rang** Harry Mazer	$2.95

Available wherever you buy books, or use this order form.